A LONG ROAD TO REDEMPTION

Tom Brewster

For information, or to order additional copies, please contact:

Beacon Publishing Group
P.O. Box 41573 Charleston, S.C. 29423
800.817.8480| beaconpublishinggroup.com

Publisher's catalog available by request.

ISBN-13: 978-1-949472-45-5

ISBN-10: 1-949472-45-5

Published in 2022. Printed in the USA.

First Edition. New York, NY 10001

Table of Contents

A LONG ROAD TO REDEMPTION

Chapter I

The 1981 IBM typewriter clattered, hammering out three sentences, then fell silent.

"Jenifer, of all those I ever loved, I loved you most," he said. A small framed woman with pale eyes and brown hair looked over her reading glasses. "My name is not Jenifer, its Theresa."

Tom read the words he had just written and ripped the paper from the typewriter, wadded it up and tossed it across the room. It bounced over the pile of other wads lying on the floor.

Molly entered the room and examined the litter. She picked up a discarded piece, smoothed it out and read it. It took her only a moment; it was only one line. She dropped it into the waste basket and picked up another crumpled sheet. In another moment she was done.

"It's hard to get started," Tom said.

"Jennifer has two *n*s," Molly said, wadding the paper and dropping it into the waste basket. She smiled a knowing smile. He really loved to write but she questioned this recent obsession. She thought he had more important things to do. He had written the novel, *The Hung Jury*, when he was a policeman, but that was 25 years ago. It had literally been on the shelf since then. Their daughter Alison found it and became interested. She was only nine years old when it was written. Now she was 34, and excited about the prospect of her dad being a writer. When she was excited about something all reason was put asunder. At this point the manuscript was in an editor's hands and nearing a publication date. She had found a website where new authors were considered, and if the writing was good enough, the manuscripts were published in a limited number, promoted on the web, and advertised at all the major book website. In the modern age of publishing anything was possible. Tom didn't have high hopes, but he did dare to fantasize about it becoming a reality.

"I've always spelled it J E N I F E R," he stated defiantly.

He believed *The Hung Jury* was a good book, but he wasn't so naïve as to think he was a Joseph Wambaugh, J.D Salinger, or the Mississippi legend John Grisham. He just thought it was good enough to be published.

It had been several years since he looked at the book, but Alison had him excited again. He read several chapters refreshing his memory and when finished he said to Molly, "It's better than I remembered." Molly wasn't one to offer false hope so when she didn't discourage him, he considered that a good sign. She was more than grounded. Sometimes she was downright pessimistic, and brutally honest. When she read it again and found it to be "not so bad," he was enthusiastic. He had been offered a deal to publish the novel by a vanity publisher back in the day before self-publishing was a taboo, but he declined, believing any book written well enough to be published should earn money, not cost money. Therefore, the book was shelved. Since then he fantasized about writing another book. but he swore he wouldn't because *The Hung Jury* had been his best effort, and if that didn't sell, nothing he wrote would. Now that Alison was involved, he was pumped up and ready for another run at it.

Molly was amused. She couldn't understand how a man who wouldn't read more than two sentences at a time would think he could write the Great American Novel. She humored him at times when he fished for compliments. At the moment she was eying some scribbling on a yellow pad lying on his desk.

"I'm like an old gray horse in the darkness waiting for the end to come."

She picked it up and scoffed, "Why do you write crap like this, it's depressing!"

"You know I have Alzheimer's - it's just a matter of time. I'm like an old horse waiting fo----"

"Stop!" Molly interrupted. "You don't have Alzheimer's."

Her eyes followed his hand as he discretely tried to cover another scrap lying there.

"Insanity cannot exist without pain. Hell is full of the wicked and uncaring who earn their way into eternal torment, but the insane innocently wander into it."

"Now where are you going to put a phrase like that in the Great American Novel?"

Tom laughed. Molly started picking up all the discarded paper.

"Why don't you use the laptop I bought you, then you could just hit the delete button after only one line. We wouldn't have all this paper lying around."

She looked around the small office. The typewriter, a small desk and two chairs nearly filled the room. It was lined with windows without curtains and some stupid looking pictures hung off center on the walls. She had attempted to change the appearance several times just to find he had changed it back upon the first opportunity. She had given up and now only entered when she wanted to clean it.

Molly was a beautiful woman. It was an old truth that when a woman possesses physical beauty in their 50's comments usually come around to *"She really looks good for her age."* Molly was beautiful not just for her 55 years, but outstanding in every way. Although she dyed her hair regularly, it was a deep natural brown and it hung across her shoulders. She threatened repeatedly to cut it, but Tom argued against it. Her hair had always been long. He liked it and wanted her to leave it as it was. She did so begrudgingly. She didn't have a wrinkle on her face and her eyes were still soft brown pools bearing a hint of green deep inside that surfaced when she was angry or excited. She was now a little heavier than she had ever been but still thin. She seemed to have a hollow leg because her weight was not proportionate to her appetite. Molly was the salutatorian in her 1968 graduating class. She should have been valedictorian, but she missed so many classes her senior year that her four-point average fell to a 3.75. She was bored with it and ready to move on and class standing had become meaningless to her. Otherwise she would have graduated number one. She wanted to go to college, but her parents didn't have the money. She had never gotten over it, but she was never bitter. Even now her mind was like a sponge. She read books and magazines continually. If there ever was a person competent to judge a novel, she was the person to do it, even over-qualified. Tom believed she was the most intelligent person he knew, but her mind worked in mysterious ways. She wasn't the easiest person in the world to get along with. Their arguments were legendary, but evidently, they had used their allotted quotient and now they just sniped at each other occasionally.

"Why don't you ever use my name in any of these stories you start but never finish?"

"Well this *J E N I F E R* (he spelled it emphasizing the single n) is in for some real heartache and emotional pain and you always find hidden meaning in everything I say. I don't want you to think I have all this animosity built up for you, *MOLLY*, he spelled her name.

"Is this your Great American Novel?"

"No."

"Then what is?" She asked with some irritation.

"You know already," he said.

"No, I don't. Anyway, if you told me I've forgotten."

He placed his glasses on the desk.

"My mom told me a story when I was a little boy. She said there was a man involved in a fight and he ran into her yard and died right in front of her."

"You can't write an entire novel based on what you just said."

Tom rolled his eyes. He was beginning to feel like he was being interrogated.

"How old was she?"

"I don't know, just a girl."

"How was he killed? Was he shot, stabbed, what happened?"

"He was shot," Tom said in a soft voice, reflective and considerate.

Molly raised her eyebrows somewhat puzzled by his tone.

"When she told me the story, she leaned her head against a wall and silently cried for just a moment. I've never forgotten that." Tom knew there was a lot more to be uncovered.

Chapter II

Tom's mother, Irene Black, was born and raised in South Central Missouri. She said she was born in Cedar Bluff, Mo., a place that cannot be found on the map. The towns in that area are Fremont, Van Buren, Dexter and Ironton. They lack any notable characteristics, but they are quaint and clean. The land is beautiful with lush forests, tree-covered mountains, and crystal-clear streams that meander through rock-filled valleys, but here in the countryside outside the communities is where the poorest inhabitants reside. Junk cars, abandoned trailer homes and run-down shanties are permanently positioned alongside the roadways. The lawns and yards sport trash piles, old refrigerators, and broken washing machines that mingle among weeds and wildflowers. Queen Ann's Lace and Black-Eyed Susan's brush up against rotting tires, rusty car parts, and discarded furniture. Little kids run shirtless and shoeless sweating with dirt rings around their necks and swim in murky ponds infested with snakes and mosquito larvae. Just to defy all reasoning, a new home will rise out of the weeds and rocks with manicured lawns, expansive landscaping and luxurious wrought-iron fencing. This was where Irene was raised.

Irene was brash and fearless, but she was also kind and intelligent. When she was young her hair was as black as a raven, and her eyes as black as coal. She was thin, willowy, and quick. She was the mother of ten kids. Tom was number five. Her father was Lawrence Black and her mother's name was Addy. She had three brothers and five sisters. Her brothers were Willy, Owen and Lester. Her sisters were Mabel, Opal, Reedy, Reva, and Louise. Irene was the oldest girl. Being the oldest came with responsibilities like washing clothes by hand on a washboard, cleaning house, chopping wood and caring for the younger children. They were laborious, exhausting tasks. She lived in conditions that would be horrific by today's standards. When she married, she found her life had not changed by degrees. She seldom mentioned her mother in an affectionate way. She scrubbed and washed clothes until her fingers bled but it was never good enough. She was usually left standing silently, never bending as she suffered harsh criticism from her mother. She never complained, but it was evident that she and her mother had a strained relationship. Tom was with her when she learned of her mother's death. She sat down quietly, and a few tears rolled down her cheek, but she was silent. After only a moment she stood up and went back to her housework without saying a word.

A Long Road to Redemption

Irene's children were Lloyd Glen, Grace Evelyn, Wanda Marie, Lawrence Emerson, Thomas A., Everett Arthur, Wilma Louise, Franklin Joseph, James Robert, and Kathleen Bonita – a lot of kids, a lot of worry.

Glen was the oldest, Tom was in the middle and Kathy was youngest. Glen was married with a two-year-old son when Kathy was born.

Irene was adored by all her children. Molly facetiously referred to her as Saint Irene but only to Tom. To speak ill of her was fighting words. Molly didn't intend it to be insulting or ridiculing and Tom didn't question her motives. He accepted it as an undeniable truth.

"So, this is a story about Saint Irene?" Molly asked.

A faraway look entered Toms eyes.

"Where are you?" she said.

He looked away.

"This is about my grandpa, and maybe about Mom," he said in a quiet voice.

Today violence and death are commonplace, and it takes something as devastating as the Columbine massacre or as catastrophic as 9/11 to captivate our attention, but in those days when Irene was a girl, murder, and hostile gunfire were proportionately larger. People were rowdy and they liked to brawl, but senseless killing was horrifying.

Even said, would the memory cause someone as sturdy as Irene to lean her head into a wall and cry, 30-plus years later? Was there another layer to the story? If there was, Tom wanted to find it. He thought it was somewhere among the iron mines, sawmills, and rocky tree-covered mountains where she was born. If he found the answer to that question it would be the basis for his Great American Novel.

"You know, most people don't even read anymore," Molly said casually, as though that alone should discourage someone from writing a book.

"You read," Tom said.

"You don't," Molly said raising an eyebrow smiling faintly.

Tom leaned back in his chair and placed his glasses back on his nose.

"Writers in the old days were perfect in their English skills and methods," Molly continued. "They had back-grounds, you know."

"Hey, I wrote *The Hung Jury*, that's background," he smiled. He knew she had his best interest at heart, but she had little faith that *The Hung Jury* would make him rich and famous or that he would ever write the Great American Novel. She picked up the wastebasket and left the room.

The wind rustled the curtains in the bathroom and the weights on the ends clinked like a wind chime. The breeze swept through the upstairs unencumbered. The large window in his office and those in the three bedrooms were open. The weather was warm, but Tom would not use the air conditioner until it was unbearably hot. He preferred the fresh air and the outside noises reverberating through the house. Tom had completely renovated the century-old home himself. Molly believed he was a better carpenter than he was a writer.

Tom was 60 years old. He had been a policeman for 14 years and an investigator for the State Attorney's Office. Now he was a private detective, licensed by the State of Illinois. He had been in his own business for 18 years. He was a fair investigator, but his business consisted of process service and filing legal documents for law offices in the region. He preferred the mundane rather than clandestine surveillances and harried witness interviews, not because it was easier but because he disliked civil suits. He hated working for lawyers, and he absolutely refused to do divorce cases. His business had been exceedingly successful for 17 years but this last year he was struggling to stay interested.

He was concerned about dropping the ball more for the welfare of his employees than anything else. Molly thought he should just sign the business over to Steve, his number one man, and come with her to Mississippi. That was another story in the making. Molly was living in Mississippi most of the time while Tom remained in Illinois running the agency. It was a business deal that required their temporary separation.

Tom sat silently looking at the keys on his typewriter. A storm was brewing on the horizon. His life was changing, with or without his consent; that was a certainty, just as the weather was taking a different turn. He watched the lightning in the distance. His mind wandered. The breeze on the curtains was increasing and he considered the coming storm. He hated storms; he had a phobia of them. It wasn't so much being in a storm but waiting for it to come. Even on a calm day he might start thinking about the weather and he could envision the sky turning black, then green, with the wind whipping leaves and hail falling from the sky. It was frightening. The absurdity of that didn't escape his recognition. When a storm finally came, it was usually anticlimactic. He retreated in his memory to a day in his childhood with an incident that was still fresh in his mind even now. That event probably contributed to his exaggerated distress. He was about five years old. On that evening it was blustery with the wind gusting, whipping dust and debris into the air with a vengeance. The sky would be dark, then clear, then dark again. The thunder rumbled in the distance then dissipated several times. When the storm finally came, darkness had descended. The sky was electrified periodically with lightning bolts illuminating everything as bright as day. The rain came in torrents. Tom stayed by his mother because he knew she was protective and strong.

If she had ever been fearful of anything, she never let anyone see it. She was like a rock in that regard. Tom's dad Willy and his oldest brother Glen were somewhere out in the storm. Irene was worried (not afraid) and she had been pacing about the house. They didn't have electricity and the kerosene lamps were totally inadequate for conditions such as those. There were six children there lined up on the davenport like a murder of crows.

Grace was the oldest, then Wanda, Lawrence, Tom, Everett and Louise who was just an infant. When the worst of the rain was over Irene gathered the kids together and dressed them to go out into the darkness. Tom didn't want to go; he wore his anxiety like a blanket, but she explained that she had to go to see about Willy and Glen. He didn't argue. None of the children ever argued with her.

They marched behind her as she traveled the long rocky lane to the low place in the creek they routinely used as a crossing. A rocky bottom made it easy to do in normal conditions, but that night it was different.

The sky was clearing, and the moon was shining through the clouds. The creek was boiling, swirling with dark muddy water. Waves rumbled past them as they stood there on the bank. Heat lightning and the moon illuminated the area as clearly as if it were midday. They looked down the creek and saw Willy's old black two-ton log truck lying on its side with water flooding through the windows, occasionally inching its way farther down the creek. Willy and Glen were standing on the opposite bank. They were soaked and muddy. Irene exchanged words with them to determine if they were alright. They were both okay. They all just stood there looking at each other for a long time. Irene shrugged her shoulders and smiled encouragingly at Willy across the creek. He waded into the water until it was chest high. He struggled to keep his feet but finally he was swept away down the raging river. He swam as hard as he could, kicking and beating against the current until he reached the safety of the other bank. Tom was panicked until he saw his dad coming out of the brush from downstream. Glen dove in head-first and paddled furiously until he was across. When all was said and done. they walked home as nothing had happened.

Many harrowing rescues have been caught on video in waters that were no more hazardous than that, with people struggling with ropes and riggings, and helicopters and rescue boats being put into motion with people shouting orders and others urgently responding. Later interviews with poor victims with quivering voices and tears flowing down their cheeks would air on TV, but that night they just walked home with Willy wondering aloud as to how they might get the truck out of the creek in the morning.

A bolt of lightning sizzled across the sky, snapping Tom back to the present. The wind swept through the house again, rustling the curtains and scattering the papers on his desk. He went to the balcony door. The wind was howling but he could see that the weather was not going to be serious. He thought again about that storm so long ago. That incident was illustrative of the Websters. They accepted life as it was handed to them. They fought determinedly against unpleasant circumstances whether it was the forces of nature, or societal conditions brought on by poverty or ill will. Tom wanted to convey that in his story. He wanted that characteristic to shine through. Facing the storm and flood was just one of the things they had to do, and they did it calmly without wavering. He admired that about his family. It caused him to wonder if someone would examine his life in retrospect and find anything admirable. He knew they would find he had been lucky. He was healthy and that was always a good thing. He had carved out a niche in law enforcement to provide a more than adequate income. His children were smart and successful. He had a great little granddaughter and another on the way.

That was all good. Although Molly was living in Mississippi she was usually home on the weekend, or else they met at their cabin in Missouri. His life had taken some strange turns along the way, but it was all good. It was too good. Tom had made mistakes that should have been fatal to his career. He was still waiting for a tsunami of calamities to even the score. Molly being in Mississippi was a little off plumb, a little out of whack, but negotiable. It would be stranger yet if people knew how he spent his evening hours: wandering around the house in his underwear drinking Kahlua and pounding on the piano in the dark. Stranger yet he couldn't read a note of music. Still, after three years living alone like this, the piano was starting to sound good. After the numerous bottles of Kahlua from a relative's wedding ran out and he learned it was 20 dollars a bottle he got off that habit. So now his bizarre behavior was limited to cruising the house in the dark in his boxers, sober, which might be more absurd. He stopped watching TV when he called the cable company complaining about the picture quality and the malevolent bastards cut him back to two local stations. That may have been a result of the pointed language he was using to describe their attitudes. They called him back on two occasions to try to resolve the problem, but he wouldn't accept. He complained about being broke and followed people around the house turning off lights and shutting doors behind them until Alison started teasing him about being the next Unabomber. She argued that he would have a hard time convincing anyone he was broke when he owned a substantial interest in a technical college, start-up shares in a bank, and property in three states. His answer was always the same. He had to race the mailman to the bank with a deposit before his checks got there.

With all the changes in his life and the changes in the hopper he was left with that one lone obsession. He liked to write. When he wrote *The Hung Jury*, he found he could describe things inside himself and attribute those characteristics to a fictional person and nobody knew it was him on the page. He could make his characters courageous and likable and honest. He could boast of his own determination and pat himself on the back without feeling guilty for his arrogance or conceit. He simply gave his best attributes to a fictional character and left out his frailties and weaknesses. It was easy and satisfying. Whether anyone ever read the words was almost insignificant. Molly didn't understand his obsession. Maybe he didn't want her to. It was so personal that he wanted to keep it to himself. The story of Irene was his secret passion.

He loved his mother and he thought there was something he should have done for her before she died that he didn't do, and it still haunted him. She wanted to talk to him about dying. She was on death's door and she needed to interact with him about it. He didn't realize at the time that when dying individuals reach the point of surrender, they need to express that to someone. She wanted to tell Tom she was ready to go. He didn't want to hear it. He encouraged her to be strong, to hang on and never give up. She died quietly and with dignity – just as she had lived. He regretted having avoided that conversation, because it is sacred and if he had it to do again, he would listen until she was exhausted, and then he would wait for her to start again. At the time he believed he wasn't worthy to enter upon that hallowed ground. Now he thought the choice was hers and he should have respected it. He should have listened.

In some strange way he thought if he could write the story she had told him when he was a child it might pay homage to her by putting her in print. He had no doubt that if he wrote a book his children would keep it forever and pass it on to their children. He believed in them totally. He wanted them to believe in her in the same way he did.

There were many things in his life he wanted to make up for that might cast aspersions on her. He was a high school dropout. Molly couldn't understand how a mother could allow her child to quit school and go out on his own as Tom had done. She loved Irene but she could not justify that one failing. Molly couldn't but Tom could and did, because he knew the whole story.

Irene had ground out a life from the harshest conditions imaginable. She was naïve about many things, but strength and resolve and bravery were her nature. She didn't know about culture and finance or society, but she knew about gumption and dignity. She knew those things were things you learned on your own. In life you reap what you sow and that was a lesson worth learning.

Tom quit school when he was 15. You might say he left head first. He punched the principal in the jaw over a heated situation where he felt he was being unfairly treated. He ended up tumbling down the stairs, having his arm twisted up behind his back, and then being shoved out the glass door, sliding face first in the cinders on the playground. Finally, he walked home wondering what he was going to do with the rest of his life.

The words burned when Tom heard them spoken. "How could she have let you quit school when you were fifteen years old?"

Tom's answer was, "Well, you had to be there."

He worked in the sawmill that winter because that was his expected vocation. He had been in the sawmill his whole life, as it was part of his family's heritage, but when he began thinking of that as his permanent position he started craving to be somewhere else. He loved the sawmill, but he wanted to see what was beyond the St. Mary's Landing city limits. He left home in good standing a month before his sixteenth birthday. Irene and Willy thought he would take a turn around the block and come right back, but he never did. He visited on a regular basis, but he was gone like a wild goose come winter.

The freedom was so good it was indescribable, but in the end, there were ramifications. You don't just ramble around without goals or responsibilities without coming to a point where you realize you've bitten yourself in the ass.

When Tom met Molly, he was 17, soon to be 18. He had knocked around doing odd jobs and worked in a pool hall for a room and bed in a space upstairs over the pool hall. In the dictionary next to *dead end* there was a picture of him. He was employed in a livestock auction house until the drunk running the place began shorting his paycheck, and finally stopped paying him altogether in lieu of having a few more bourbon and cokes. On his last day he was promised a paycheck that never came. He then went to the Hiram Walker stave mill. He was living in Delavan, Illinois and hitching a ride to work in Hopedale. Hiram Walker was where he belonged. Poor people in Missouri where he was born gravitated to sawmills and logging operations and stave mills. That's where they were supposed to stay. On the smart ladder he was one rung above dumbass. The problem was that he had the audacity to become enamored with Molly. He knew enough even being one rung removed that a beautiful girl like her wouldn't be interested in him, if she knew he was a high school dropout earning minimum wage. He had already lost his hillbilly accent and spent everything he earned on clothes to keep himself looking like any other middle-class teenager. He would have lied if she had asked him about school, but she didn't. His deception was so complete that she didn't know he had quit school until they had been married for over two years.

The shame was that he had never intended to be dishonest. He had fallen into a self-constructed snare. He thought he would date her for a while, she would learn his deficiencies and he would go off with a broken heart and that would be the end of it. He would grow old and toothless with sawdust in his hair and in his shoes and would forever be harmless.

He hoped he could just fit in for a while. He carried a copy of Rudyard Kipling's poem, "If," in his back pocket for years as an incentive to be upright, considerate and strong. It was all the advice needed for a son or a daughter, and a guide to live by. There was nothing in it to help a floundering hillbilly boy to get out of a jam. It wasn't a malicious conniving deceit, but a small lie out of control.

Molly was bright and studious. She was a cheerleader and probably the best-looking girl in Delavan high school. She should have taken one look at him and ran. In life there is fate, ill fate and destiny. There is another condition too. It's called irony. Tom's life had become a cascading, tumbling smack of irony. He had never intended to become a police officer, especially under fraudulent conditions. A friend he had known for a few years was recruited by the police department. He was attending the police academy in Champaign, Illinois. The department was testing to add three more officers. The friend brought Tom an application and he filled it out and returned it. He left the educational background blank. The detective who was assigned to Tom's background investigation was retiring and had become lackadaisical. He okayed the application without even looking at it.

Tom was astounded when he was called for an interview. He was dumbfounded and in disbelief, but he went through the process because he didn't want to tell his friend that he was a high school dropout. 130 applicants made the cut and Tom was number one (so much for psychological testing.) He accepted the position for the same reason he had taken the test: he didn't want to admit to his friend or to Molly that he had quit school. As bizarre as it was, he became a police officer in a state where the minimum requirement was a high school diploma. After graduating from the police academy, the department required his attendance in a report-writing class at the local college. When he enrolled he was given a short form from the Department and never asked about his high school record, so he continued to enroll in classes until he graduated. He graduated first in the social science division. Tom went on to become the best police officer he could be, but behind it he felt like an imposter.

In 1976 Tom arrested Russell Parker, a Willoughby Hills College student, for shoplifting. As it turned out, he was a sociopath who promptly went about murdering the witnesses to his misdemeanor. Tom wrote *The Hung Jury* based upon the circumstances of that case.

By that time Tom had forgotten he was no more than a sawmill hand and one rung above dumbass. To find his way to that position without a high school diploma was highly unlikely. The process is long and tedious. They look at every detail of an applicant's life. They question neighbors, friends and pour over their backgrounds thoroughly. The state prohibits hiring an applicant who does not have a high school diploma. This was clearly a house of cards. Now that he was a private detective he was earning many times more money than he had earned as a police officer, but here too, the State of Illinois requires five years as a police officer, one year as an investigator plus two years college or a four year college degree. It worried him because he just didn't know if having quit school would negate all the other requirements. Molly thought he was crazy to worry about it when he was sixty years old. In an insane way he thought if he wrote well enough and became a published author he might somehow be vindicated. But there was another aspect to his desire to write. Something deep inside that he could not explain. He just wanted to bleed his emotions out upon the world.

There are forces beyond explanation. Destiny, fate, and ill fate would be directed by God or by a higher power, but irony is just a tumbling along of things in sequence that finally in the end you say, *"How in hell did that happen!"* This surely was irony. Now, *The Hung Jury* was going to print, and he had never been caught in all his deceit. While he waited for its failure, or success, he would submerge himself in his new effort. He and Molly called it his Great American Novel. What a grandiose notion!

Chapter III

Molly was living in Mississippi. Tom was living in Illinois. If they weren't already the odd couple, they would at least do until the real odd couple arrived. They found themselves involved in the queerest of circumstances. Their lives were fragmented by time and distance. They had invested in property along with their daughter Alison and son-in-law Rod Miller. Both Alison and Rod were Willoughby Hills College employees. Rod was a vice president and Alison in the recruiting department. A friend, Brian Huffman, CEO of Mid Illinois Technical Institute, was looking for a location to expand his educational facilities in 2005. Alison got wind of it and put a plan into motion. She moved to Southaven, Mississippi, acquired a real estate license and found a suitable place to establish a school. She was there several months selling houses while Rod remained at Willoughby Hills College. Eventually she approached Tom and Molly to make an investment. After some apprehension, arguing and back-peddling they agreed. They bought the property and leased to Midwest Technical Institute, a charter was formed, and Mississippi Technical College was launched. Rod and Alison were part of the bargain. Rod was named president and Alison chief financial officer. It was born in chaos and frenzy. Alison became pregnant, employees were impossible to find and keep and during the only hard freeze they had in Mississippi that year the pipes froze throughout the entire main building and destroyed several classrooms. Eventually the baby was born. Adison Royal Miller ushered in new light, and along with her, new hope. Employees were acquired who could read, write and do arithmetic, and Molly moved to Mississippi to help with the baby, then finally to join the college as an administrator. Tom stayed in Illinois in his underwear playing the piano in the evenings and conducting his legal support business by day.

Although they lived in different locations, they spent weekends together either at their cabin in Missouri, or one or the other would make the drive between Mississippi and Illinois. Molly was taking a break from school so on July 13th, they were in Willoughby Hills packing for a trip to Missouri to do a cursory investigation into the "dead man incident". That was now the phrase they routinely used when they were referring to the story Irene had related to Tom when he was a little boy. It was a trip Molly definitely did not want to make, but she had *suggested* it hoping he would decline and put an end to his ridiculous yearning. He accepted gratefully knowing she would rather have her teeth pulled out and admired that she could smile while it happened. She might just have a little saint in her too.

They usually went to Cocoa Beach for their vacations where they had several timeshare weeks, but that was being forfeited for the "dead man" research for the Great American Novel. Molly recalled his earlier description of insanity. It called for pain. She would endorse that at this point. It was insane to take this trip, and she was indeed feeling the pain. Their son Ryan and his wife Stephanie were driving down from Milwaukee to join them. Tom realized Molly's pain. She did not suffer quietly and several times he reminded her that it was her idea, but to compensate he suggested they first drive to Southaven to spend two days with Alison and Rod before jumping headfirst into their folly. She accepted cheerfully knowing it would reduce the time allotted to the "dead man" investigation.

Tom and Molly were opposite in nearly every way. Time and space were not the only obstacles between them. Tom thought about infinity and how long it might last. Molly thought about the wash and if there might have been a groan in the washing machine. Tom drove along in his car seeing the beauty of the hills and the grass and the fields. Molly watched the gas gauge. Tom commented on how well the car was taking the curves, and he thought about writing the Great American Novel. Molly shook her head and smiled about his spelling. They should have been incompatible, but they weren't. They had been married for 38 years and although they were apart now, they were alloyed together. They were like steel: stronger as two components than as individuals.

As they readied for the trip Molly was finishing her packing. "Have you packed everything?" she asked.

"Yes."

"Do you have your shaving kit?"

"Oh, hell, I don't," he said, looking around the room for the brown leather bag.

Molly cocked her head and gave him the look. She knew he didn't have it, but she was testing him. All women are sisters in that regard.

"Do you have extra shoes?"

"Yep," he lied, fetching a pair from the closet sheepishly.

She started inspecting his bags.

"You know I have Alzheimer's, so why torture me. Just tell me what you want me to take," he laughed. "I'll remember long enough to get the things you tell me to get."

"You don't have Alzheimer's," she snapped.

She zipped her bag and banged it onto the floor. He picked it up and took it along with his to the car.

When he returned Molly was reading a fax she had retrieved from the fax machine.

"Did you talk to Donna Webster about your grandpa – about the dead man incident?" She asked perusing the memo. She always called Donna by both her first and last name as if there were too many Donnas in the world for him to guess which Donna she was talking about.

Donna Webster had sent pictures, but that wasn't what he wanted. They were old and black and white with little significance to his research.

He confessed; he had called her about an article written about the "dead man incident". He had also called his sisters, Louise and Kathy, and Joe's wife, Mary. Molly didn't call Mary by both names as she did Donna Webster, although there are also many Marys which might cause equal confusion.

He was looking for the newspaper article they had passed around at a family gathering a few years ago. It described an event from the 1930's. He didn't remember who brought the article or the newspaper in which it was printed, the date or anything else which might identify it, but he remembered the contents. The victim was described as a well-known bully and troublemaker who got what was coming to him. It could not have been stated more clearly if it had said THE WILL OF GOD WAS EXECUTED UPON LOCAL EVILDOER! The longer version was that two men, brothers-in-law, were drunk and unruly throughout the day. The man who eventually suffered the ill fate was the instigator. He chased his cohort from two beer joints during the escalating calamity. It took several hours to unfold but finally the mean bastard assumed ground temperature.

The newspaper described all of that in much more detail, but in the final paragraph it said the dead man was wearing a bullet from a rare gun, and Lawrence Black, Tom's grandfather and the lone witness to the incident, was the only person in the county to have such a gun. This was the "dead man incident" in a nutshell.

Donna Webster also had information that this same man had followed Irene and her sisters from school, leering and uttering obscene remarks – a clear motivation for Lawrence to have a grudge against him.

The dead man article was discussed at that family gathering and the consensus was formed that perhaps their grandfather had been the shooter but somehow, he escaped being accused. The newspaper could not have stated it more clearly. Now Tom was trying to locate a copy to learn what newspaper had printed it. He was discreetly trying to find it. Nobody in the family knew he had written *The Hung Jury*, or that he was now pursuing a new endeavor. He had never told them about writing a book, and he had no intention of telling them about it now. When the book came out, they would know then. He thought they would think it was pure foolishness. Something like Gilligan running around the island taking notes and interviewing Thurston B. Howell III and the professor for the novel he would never write. Sometimes he felt like an intruder there, so he compartmentalized everything. When he was with family, he wasn't the same man he was in his other life. Disclosing that he had written a book and was researching for another was out of the question.

Molly thought they were all proud of him. He had grabbed life like a bucking bull, by the horns, hanging tough all alone until it came around to his terms. They thought he was rich and knew things they didn't know. But that was her opinion. He didn't have that same confidence. He was grateful they were proud of him, but he believed he was still that middle child in the pecking order who bumped around the others avoiding trouble. The things he had done that were a true source of pride were unknown to the others. Such as graduating from college, even if it was somewhat illegitimate. He had never informed them that he was a college graduate. Now he wanted to write the Great American Novel, but it wasn't likely he would put that out for family scrutiny either.

Molly, a woman who loved him dearly, didn't believe in the Great American Novel, so how could they? And was it audacity to think he could deliver on such a grandiose endeavor? Would there be a smirk behind a tight little smile, "Did he just say he was writing a book?"

Ryan and Stephanie finally arrived sporting a new car – a Dodge Nitro. Stephanie was five months pregnant and her convertible wouldn't fit the family plan. The new black SUV was offered up for transportation. After transferring their bags to the new car, they were "off to see the wizard," a phrase Tom had uttered redundantly over the years.

Tom's brothers and sisters, all but Grace, still lived in St. Mary's Landing, Missouri. He frequently stopped there when traveling between Willoughby Hills and Southaven. Today they would find themselves there as part of their trip.

Coming into town was depressing inasmuch as the streets were deserted and the buildings were mostly vacant. Once-stoic red brick homes standing atop rolling hills with green lawns were now in disrepair. The Mississippi River had raged into the streets once too often, destroying businesses and homes, finally washing away all desire to save it. In Tom's lifetime there had been four floods inundating the town, 1953, 1972, 1992 and 1995. There were still a few shops and homes on the east side of Main St., but they were sparse and in decay.

The Saline River runs along the east side of St, Mary's while a rusty abandoned railroad occupies the back side of the dilapidated buildings and a rotten hulking feed mill overlooks the river. Willow trees stand in groves upon an embankment that descends from the tracks to the water, covered with rocks and debris. An iron bridge spans the Saline River to Kaskaskia Island. Beyond that rich farm ground stretches to Mississippi River.

During the 30s and 40s, St. Mary's Landing was a vibrant progressive community. There were 620 people listed on the population sign, but it was larger by the fact all the farm community was attracted there to shop and socialize. The Mississippi was like a bulldozer when it was out of its banks. It destroyed everything in its path. St. Mary's Landing was decimated. Businesses and residents found it easier to relocate than to battle the river. The Websters had been there since Tom was in second grade, and they accepted the Mississippi, whether it was raging or simply flowing along.

Tom pointed to a vacant lot where the doctor's office had been, along with the variety store, the feed store and the several taverns which now were just ghosts in his memory. The old hotel where the Websters lived was gone and another small house they occupied was an empty lot; yet another had only the basement walls left standing.

Molly was amused. She had seen it all before. Ryan was absorbed and fascinated. He had been there many times as a child, but his interest had not waned. Tom imagined that he listened with a different ear now that his own child was on the way. Ryan loved hearing about the hard times, the fighting and the struggles. He saw Tom as an all-American hero overcoming injustice and inequity. Tom liked that too, even as exaggerated as it was. Stephanie was astounded. Her family was middle-class Wisconsin dwellers who lived in clean, well-kept surroundings. This was her first trip to Tom's boyhood home.

They drove through town on old Route 61, seeing empty lots on both sides of the street; intersections with stop signs for traffic that no longer passed through; and sidewalks and steps leading to houses that were no longer there. They rounded the curve on the south end of town and headed out into the country. The sawmill was coming into sight and the smell of sawdust was in the air. It was that old familiar fragrance, a smell so sweet it was forever seeded in Tom's memory. That smell permeated his childhood. His youth was filled with long summer days playing in the log yard, in the lumber yard and around the mill. It was a time when he didn't know he was poor, or that there was another world and another life away from his little town. Everything was in sync and everything mattered. His dad was the Mill Sawyer. He was the supervisor and administrator and had final say on everything about the operation. He just didn't make much money. If the weather prohibited the mill from running, he didn't make anything. No work, no pay. There was so much responsibility for so little reward, but it was a way of life.

Glen owned the mill now and their brother Joe ran the operations. It was much more prosperous than it was when Willy was in charge. There had been a Webster in that mill for over seventy years. The way Glen and Joe churned out the money you wouldn't be able to convince the people in St. Mary's Landing this was a dead end or a repository for the poor.

They drove into the log yard, bouncing across the ruts left by the loaders and skidders. Bark and sawdust covered the ground. Only a few logs were lying haphazardly about, leaving the place looking empty. The mill was idle with only one lone employee shoveling sawdust and debris away from the skids. The office door was open, but nobody was there.

They stopped and Tom talked to the employee. It was 90 degrees and he was dressed in heavy brown coveralls. His baseball cap covered his head, but wild wiry hair escaped, protruding in all directions. His large blue eyes darted about like a man who was trying to come up with a lie but didn't have the aptitude for it. At any rate, he was more talented at rolling his eyes around in his sockets than speaking the English language.

"Where is everybody?" Tom asked.

"Gone. Kain't get no logs," he answered in a high-pitched nasally voice. "We're shet down."

"Where's Glen and Joe?"

"Gone to the woods. Glen bought timber and he's gonna brang it in hisself. Him'n Joe." Tobacco juice ran down his chin and dripped onto his chest.

It was becoming more difficult to buy logs in recent years. It was their biggest problem in the operation. Glen didn't think it had anything to do with shortages in trees, but Tom reserved some doubt. However, he never questioned Glen. It wasn't his place to be dubious. Glen was 70 and nobody ever had to motivate him to find ways to make money. The logging operation was usually handled by employees but today he and Joe were bringing in the timber.

Earlier, Tom got directions from the employee who pointed a great deal, making statements like "go that a way, and turn this way," as though he thought Tom might be able to see through the several miles beyond and into the heavily forested hills. With a little patience, which he usually didn't have a great reserve of, they had a flight plan.

They stopped at a gas station and bought beer while en route. The bottles clinked in the box as they navigated tops from felled trees and parked machinery on the narrow logging road.

When they reached the logging site Glen was the only one there. He was sitting atop the loader operating the levers systematically. Skillfully, he guided the steel arm and claw fetching logs from various locations and placed them onto the truck bed. Glen watched the new arrivals bouncing down the road but didn't go to greet them. He continued working until all the trucks were loaded.

Tom and Ryan were already having a beer while Molly and Stephanie talked about the possibility of bugs and snakes creeping up on them.

Glen climbed down from the loader, scrutinizing them with a blank expression as he often did. He had a way of looking at a person like a man who might be studying everything about you before he would venture a remark. After he looked everyone over thoroughly, he smiled.

"Where's all your help?" Tom asked

"Hell, Joe fired all our Mexicans!" He laughed.

They employed several Mexicans from an employment agency and things had gotten slightly out of hand. The problem was that Jose Garcia might be a different person each week. Same name, same Social Security Number, same mailing address, but a different face. It was hard to find any one of them to answer to the names they were using.

"They all showed up yesterday and we didn't know any of 'em. They said they were Jose, Ramon, Jorge and Rafael. Joe sent 'em packing," he laughed. It was a pathetic situation and he knew it. Tom laughed, as he knew the situation too. They had a bunkhouse where the Mexicans lived but they came and went when the train ran, leaving their Social Security cards and identifications. The next man in became whomever his bunk had been assigned to before him. When the work was simple Joe ignored the changing faces, but here in the woods the machinery was huge and complicated. Someone who had never seen a loader surely couldn't operate one.

"What's going on?"

"We're on our way to Memphis," Tom answered.

"You're keeping poor company," Glen said, smacking Ryan's stomach with his open hand. Glen liked Ryan. He was rambunctious and daring. He was always ready to try anything, and nothing scared him. He was similar to his Uncle Glen in that respect.

Ryan climbed the ladder to the skidder and examined the gears and levers.

"Ryan, you don't know how to work that thing," Molly warned. She often forgot he was 32 years old and a married man. He was still that reckless little boy to her and qualified for constant worry.

"He can't hurt anything," Glen said, keeping an eye on Ryan perched high in the air in the skidder seat.

Ryan turned the key and the diesel engine turned over several times before smoke puffed out the exhaust. The motor roared and the skidder came to life. Stephanie suppressed an alarmed squeal. Ryan pushed it into gear and slowly surged forward.

Glen watched Stephanie's eyes, which were focused on Ryan, waiting for him to screw himself into a bleeding unidentifiable mass.

Glen snickered, knowing Ryan was safe astride the hulking machine, amused by Stephanie's reaction.

"Ryan, you're gonna kill yourself up there," she shouted. Ryan smiled and killed the switch.

"He can't hurt anything," Glen assured her.

"He could turn it over and kill himself," she argued. She was smiling at her own hysteria.

"He couldn't turn it over if he tried."

Glen was very active and in excellent condition for his 70 years.

A Long Road to Redemption

Ryan jumped to the ground and Glen took his turn in the seat. He cranked the diesel up and pointed it towards a large log pile. The tires on the skidder were probably six to eight feet tall and to climb over a single log was a paltry feat. He scaled one after another on his way to the larger endeavor just for practice. He ran at the log pile with wheels churning. He was like a granddaddy longlegs climbing a pile of twigs. The logs moved and wobbled underneath the wheels, tilting the skidder sideways, but then the wheels would drop down still churning and pulling, sailing the skidder sideways with a jolt.

Stephanie laughed and covered her mouth. "He's crazy."

The skidder bobbed and weaved, laying nearly over on its side then recovered. Glen took off his cap and waved like a cowboy on a bucking bronco.

Molly said, "You're right. He is crazy," but she smiled her wry little smile. The same smile she exposed when she was amused by something ridiculous.

Tom thought to himself, "He's not crazy, but he is a fearless son-of-a-bitch." It was just one of the things he admired about his older brother. When Tom was ten years old the Websters were the poorest family in a poor town. Most people in St. Mary's Landing were poor too, but they knew there was always somebody poorer than they were. It was the Websters. Glen strutted around like he owned the entire place. He rubbed elbows with the richest people there, and there were a few, and he was never intimidated. He had taken the mill, which was a traditional backbreaker, and become wealthy. He and Joe had both prospered. When their dad ran the mill, they were laid flat on poverty's door. Glen had changed all that. Now he was the man, and he liked it.

The skidder continued to mount the log pile until it roosted, superlatively idle atop the 20 feet tall log pile with Glen smiling back at those still on the ground. After savoring the victory, he descended the pile then put up against a medium-sized tree, raised the blade and pushed it to the ground. Tom, Ryan and Stephanie laughed, and Molly smiled her passive little smile. Glen was quite lofty astride his splendid machine. He grinned, convinced he had given them a good show. He parked the skidder then trotted back to the others.

Without taking a moment to evaluate his recent activity he pointed to Stephanie's stomach. "You're in a family way!" He said.

She was mortified but forced a grin. She had met Glen before but here he was in his own element here in the woods. He was brash and mischievous.

"Yes, I'm getting fat right through here," she said, turning her hands out, fanning across her thighs and hips.

"You won't lose it either," he bantered.

"You shut up, you're making the baby mad," she laughed. She was starting to get it. You were never left on the sidelines when your name was Webster.

They all sat down on a log and Tom dispensed the beer. Ryan questioned Glen's judgment in drinking on the job. Glen just said he would drink if he wanted to, he was the boss.

Soon their conversation turned to family history. Tom started asking Glen about the "dead man incident". His motivation was to uncover clues. Ryan was curious too. Tom had given him fragmented tales but never anything concrete. They thought Glen would have the real story but getting to it without going through the other Webster legends was the problem.

Willy Webster was a quiet hard-working man without skills beyond the sawmill industry. Glen contended that the Websters were impoverished because Pop wasn't a smart businessman.

"He worked hard, not smart," Glen said.

The proof was in the pudding in that Glen and Joe were doing exactly the same business and the money was there to be had.

The quiet hardworking part about Pop wasn't their usual topic of discussion. Willy had a quiet exterior but inside he was an agitated, dangerous man. Inside he was fuming like a pressure cooker rumbling with a loose lid. When his fury found a route, he erupted in unimaginable violence and anger. This was the part they liked to talk about. It was funny to them. The Websters weren't politically correct and were amused by his conduct. They entertained each other by frequently rehashing his violent antics.

They all seemed to have one event they owned. Tom's was the baseball bat encounter he had with a neighborhood youth. When he was ten years old, he was in the road batting rocks with a 29-inch Louisville Slugger. The field across the street was occupied by Bill Hamilton's hogs so no human life was in jeopardy.

Willy and Gilbert Madison were in the side yard engaged in a congenial conversation. Gilbert was 22, strong, athletic, black and moderately militant. Just two days prior he had been involved in a fight with two cousins, Butch and Lewis Coffman. Reports from neighborhood kids who had seen the fight depicted a row that was no less than savage. Butch and Lewis were not troublemakers, but they were tough, strong, hard teenagers. There was punching, kicking, elbowing, grunting and profanity not heard in purgatory or hell. Two dogs were tearing at Gilbert's pant legs and dust hovered in the air and mingled with spit and blood. In the end Butch was left groaning in the ditch and Lewis ran off into a field. Gilbert wasn't afraid of a fight.

The Websters had seldom used an inside toilet or garnered a thought of having one in their house. On a whim Pop decided they would step into the 20th century. He employed Gilbert to dig a hole in the back yard six feet square and six feet deep. It was a perfect sized hole for a septic tank. Gilbert agreed to do the job for six dollars. In 1960 six dollars was more valuable than in 2009, but even then, a hole like that was a bargain for that price.

It was mid-summer, the heat was intense, and the air was heavy. Gilbert sweated, huffed and puffed and worked like a machine for two days. When he was finished there was a beautiful six feet square hole in the yard. The sides were straight and smooth. The floor was wet and muddy, but certainly level. It truly was an excellent hole.

When he was finished Pop brought out the garden hose (they had an outside spigot, the first running water they ever had,) and hosed the mud and dirt off Gilbert's back. Gilbert was appreciative and the two men were enthusiastic about the hole and pleased with the endeavor. Things turned sour when the settlement came. Pop gave Gilbert the six dollars they had agreed upon. Gilbert looked at the money for a long moment lying in his open palm. He had an expression like a man who had been splashed by a motorist while he was dressed in his Sunday suit. It was pure pain and disappointment.

"I'ze thank'n that job'd be wurth moran nat, Mr. Willy," Gilbert said with a definite air of irritation.

Pop realized instantly that the merriment was over.

"That's what you're gett'n," Pop said looking Gilbert straight in the eyes.

Gilbert had just come off the championship neighborhood fight, so he wasn't about to back down from a skinny little gray-haired man with a limp.

"Now come on, Mr. Willy, You know that job's wurth morn nat!"

Pop's bottom lip tightened but he spoke soft and low. "It may be," he paused for a long moment while his signature anger percolated, "But that's what you're getting. We agreed on six dollars!" His eyebrows raised and bristled. At that point Gilbert puffed out his chest and cocked his head. He screwed his face into the most tormented expression ever known to mankind. At first his voice came out in a squeak like a teakettle coming to a boil; then it burst into the air with ferocity.

"You're a goddamn liar, you old gray wolf, son-of-a-bitch!"

Tom froze in his tracks. Pop reached out and snatched the baseball bat from his hand and spun around with the bat raised and cocked. Gilbert saw what was coming and turned his head to avoid being struck straight in the face. Pop swung from his heels and struck Gilbert in the back of his head! The crack was so loud the pigs in the field jumped and stirred to make an escape. The bat splintered leaving Pop with only a 12-inch handle. Gilbert was still on his feet, but his legs were like two rubber bands. His head and arms were trying to go straight but his feet were taking him sideways. Pop ran after him and plunked him in the back with the remaining stubby handle. Gilbert's eyes were glazed but finally he focused, and his feet picked up the speed. His legs had returned, and he was bounding like a gazelle taking eight feet strides as he went. Pop walked back towards the house muttering and breathing heavily. Six 1-dollar bills were strewn upon the ground.

"Come back, you son-of-a-bitch, I'll give you the six bucks I owe you!"

He went into the house and never mentioned the incident again. Three or four months later they filled in the hole.

The thing that astonished Tom was that Willy wasn't concerned that he might have killed Gilbert. It's very likely that a baseball bat across the head will kill most people. Miraculously, there is a gray-haired old Gilbert Madison walking around today and he talks about the incident as if it were a party trick.

Willy Webster was a kind man in every way except for in those moments when his anger ruled his judgment. To be acquainted with him didn't mean that you knew him. To be acquainted with him was to see a non-judgmental small-framed man with a body that was deteriorated and defined by a limp he ferried in from youth. He never gossiped or condemned, and he was easy to be around, but in those instants when that astounding rage glazed over his eyes and he unhinged from reality, those acquainted with him realized they had never known him. In that moment he was a stranger even to himself. When the Webster family talked about the seething rampages, they laughed about it, but even when he lay dying if he had gotten up and glazed over, they would have all looked for a hiding place. The one exception would have been Irene. She had no fear and she never turned away.

The stories about Willy's wild antics and Irene's bravery would have taken up the entire afternoon but Tom wanted to know about the dead man incident. He wanted that newspaper article. He knew it was his lifeline to uncovering the truth.

"Where is the article about Grandpa Black?" he asked Glen.

"Why are you looking for that?"

Tom didn't want to admit he was researching the incident for a book. If he had been endorsed by Charles Dickens from the grave he wouldn't have confessed. He didn't want to insinuate to anyone that he thought he was a serious writer. If there were legs on his dream, then the fate of *The Hung Jury* and the great American novel would be left to himself and strangers.

Glen didn't know any more about the article than Tom. He learned that none of his sisters knew either. It was frustrating but he believed he would eventually find it somewhere else, and he wasn't giving up.

After a few more beers their thoughts and discussion meandered away from the dead man incident to more mundane matters. They were only halfway to Memphis, and it was mid-afternoon. A few goodbyes and they were off again.

Chapter IV

Tom was quiet in the back seat. It was foreign to him. When he was a policeman he was never partnered up and he never spent time in the passenger seat. He had driven a million miles in his life, but he was seldom in a vehicle without being behind the wheel.

In the back seat he surveyed the scenery, watching the fence post sweeping by, and the green fields and cliffs carved out of the rocks alongside the road. The sky was clear, but it was afternoon and the sunlight in the hills cast oblique rays onto the objects manifesting in a golden hue. The wildflowers were more brilliant, and they strayed into the trees and the fences and lined up against the roadside. They were golden, yellow, red and blue. The Queen Ann's Lace stood peeking out over them, swaying in the breeze.

Molly watched out the window too, quietly thinking. She may have appeared to be admiring the flowers, but Tom understood her and knew she could not appreciate wildflowers no matter how beautiful. They were things that could not be controlled. She saw them as invaders and rebels. They were to be supplanted and destroyed. She loved violets, lilies, roses, impatiens and mums, but those foreign intruders were trespassers and vandals. They came in from the fields and alleys and on the breeze. Even here in the wilderness their mere existence concerned her.

"Wooly!" she exclaimed.

Tom smiled a knowing smile.

"Were you disappointed?" she queried.

"We didn't learn anything," he admitted.

Molly watched his face. She was searching his expression for a sign.

"What?" he asked.

She just shook her head.

"You think this is all folly," he said quietly, keeping the conversation from Ryan and Stephanie in the front seat.

"No secrets back there," Stephanie piped. "You're making the baby mad," she muttered in a whisper. She used the expression so many times now that she was embarrassed, but she couldn't stop.

"No, I don't think it's folly, but this glorification of violence – I don't get it. What story is there? Are you wanting your grandfather to have been the shooter?"

"I want to know the truth," he paused. "You know, there's been so much violence in my life I could write a book about what I saw before I was 12. But this - this is a mystery. I would like to know. I'd like to write about it."

Molly stared out the window. She wanted to say more but feared to tread farther.

"Go on," he said.

"If you're doing this as a hobby, then, good. Have some fun; but if you're banking on The Great American Novel or even *The Hung Jury*, well – I just don't want to see you disappointed, that's all."

Now Tom looked out the window. He was frustrated. It wasn't a hobby and he wasn't banking on it but he wanted to dream.

"*The Hung Jury* was a good book," Molly added, "And if it had been written by a well-known writer there's no doubt it would be successful, but what are the odds? Well, I'm just saying—" She stopped in mid-sentence having nothing more to add.

I-55 came into view and they made the ramp and headed south. It wasn't long before they were in cotton country. The six-pack Ryan had bought was consumed in the woods and they wanted to replenish their supply and buy wine to take to Rod and Alison's. Molly wasn't drinking and being pregnant, Stephanie couldn't consume alcohol. As a result, Tom and Ryan were now relegated to the back seat to rehash family history.

They stopped in Steele, Missouri, six miles north of the Missouri-Arkansas state line. After some complaining about the time spent in the car and some mention about flying next time, they found a gas station with beer and wine. Tom went inside while the others waited, stretching and yawning. When he came back, he had several wine bottles and a 12-pack.

"There were some "screely" looking people in there," he said, smiling at Molly, knowing she would respond to his description.

"Alright, Lucille," she laughed.

"Screely" was a fabricated word he had picked up from Molly's mom. He liked to use it to torment Molly. Those who fit the description may have had many characteristics undesirable to her mother, Lucille. "Screely" was a word that would encapsulate those traits that didn't have a clear definition. They were people who might somehow have slithered into a public place unnoticed or slipped up silently behind you, breathing noticeably, just barely within your hearing in an annoying way. They may have possibly sweated through their clothing and then continued to wear them after they had dried. They would have sunken chests and their hair would have been combed wet with strands stuck together and flattened against their heads. They would be unsubstantial in many ways but "screely" was the perfect description.

These "screely" looking people did not elicit sympathy, "Oh, that poor screely looking soul!" It was always something like, "That screely-looking fool doesn't know when to come in out of the rain!" Or, "That screely-looking thing can't be trusted."

It was as though the "screely"-looking people were "screely"-looking by their own design simply to make others uneasy by their mere presence.

As pathetic as it was Tom had incorporated the word into his vocabulary.

"There's some "screely" looking Websters too," Molly mused. Her way of getting back at him.

"That may be true, but we started this county," Tom said.

Stephanie had been quiet until then.

"What?" She chirped.

"Yep, William Webster founded the Plymouth Bay Area Colony."

"Are you kidding me? Are you related?"

"You're a Webster too," Tom stated in an accusing way, as though she might be part of his "screely-looking family tree.

"I don't know, after hearing all those Webster stories," she teased. "And what about the dead man incident you keep talking about!"

"That's the Black side," he said. "I mean the family Black. Not the dark side, not to be confusing."

"You know the first man hung in America was a Webster," Ryan piped in.

They all laughed. The truth was that the man involved in the Plymouth Bay area colony was

William Brewster, and the first man hung in American was a Brewster, not a Webster.

Later when it was nearing darkness. they crossed the Mississippi river into Tennessee. The Memphis skyline was visible, and Molly pointed out the pyramid and noted that it was the largest in the world. The Memphis skyline was fairly nondescript with the exception of the giant pyramid. A few tall buildings jutted into the magenta sky, but nothing unmistakably Memphis. The greatest assets in Memphis were not the sights, but the sounds. Crossing over the Mississippi River, the low hum of the blues hung heavy in the air like a primal hunger at dusk. They discussed stopping and doing Beale St., but then decided to go on to Hernando to Rod and Alison's.

Tom made his usual comment about Memphis people believing erroneously that Memphis is larger than St. Louis. He argued that the St. Louis metro area was much bigger than Memphis. It was a statistic he could not produce, but he was adamant. Molly made her usual comment that the St. Louis downtown was bigger, but she thought Memphis was the bigger of the two cities. They stuck to their arguments.

Tom had lived in St. Louis briefly in his trek across time and had fallen in love with the city. He lived in a poor neighborhood near the Soulard district.

He was a Cardinals fan and kept his car radio tuned to KMOX at all times. Even now he listened when the reception permitted. St. Mary's Landing is seventy-five miles south of St. Louis, not part of the metro area, but certainly near enough to be influenced by it. Both newspapers sold in St. Mary's Landing were from St. Louis and KMOX was the only radio station they could hear. He knew everything about St. Louis. It was definitely his big town.

Soulard Market was only a few blocks from where he stayed while he was there. On Saturday mornings he would go to the market to soak up the atmosphere. The people meandering about were from all walks of life. Some came for the fresh vegetables; others for the gourmet meat, and still some were there for the bratwursts and beer. There were always street entertainers, fiddlers, guitarist, banjo players and sometimes even bagpipes. The place had grown in diversity since the arrival of thousands of immigrants from Europe and Asia. Memphis was Molly's big city now, but Soulard's Market was still her favorite place to stop in between Willoughby Hills and Memphis. The Soulard district was where Tom's free fall began. It was where he experienced the fitful feeling that is present only in youth that affixes inside the body somewhere and moves with excitement across, up and down and throughout every nerve within. It's a feeling that comes with growing up but is enhanced by being free. It's fearing or being apprehensive about what might be around the corner but being so excited by the prospect that it causes an internal fluttering that is both uncomfortable and pleasant, punctuated by surges of unbridled exuberance. Tom loved St. Louis for that reason and especially Soulard.

They continued to banter each other good-naturedly about the two cities. Molly loved the south. She swore she would never return to Willoughby Hills to live. Memphis was definitely her big city now.

Mississippi Technical College is in Southaven, Mississippi. Rod and Alison's home was in Hernando. The college is on State Line Rd. where Memphis city limits begin. Molly lived with Alison and Rod during the week but on the weekend, she was on the road between Willoughby Hills and Hernando. She had her own room and bathroom and if she chose to, she could spend all her time alone. Her bedroom was 14 by 24, which is as large as some people have in an entire apartment. She worked from 7:00 a.m., to 2:30 p.m. at Mississippi Tech. Her title was compliance manager. She was the rules lady. After 2:30 she was with her granddaughter, Adison Royal Miller. Adi was 2 ½ years old. She had blond hair, blue eyes and the most intelligent-looking face God ever sent down the pike.

Stephanie had driven the entire trip. She seemed tired but cheerful. They drove into the Lakes of Cedar Grove right on time. The expansive lawns were lush and green with diverse landscaping spreading out before lavish brick homes. The streets were divided by a median with roses, impatiens and geraniums. The roundabout and the curb lines were as much for aesthetics as they were for traffic calming. Each time Tom visited Mississippi he marveled at the extravagant homes and the stylish business facilities. "Where were all the poor people?"

He and Molly had driven throughout the area and found the towns to be clean and upscale, having the appearance of being upper income. Even the neighborhoods with smaller, more economic houses were well-kept. This was not the Dixie he had heard about. His own hometown, Willoughby Hills, Illinois, seemed backward compared to Hernando and Southaven.

Alison and Rod's home was bright with all the lights glowing in the night. Adison squealed with excitement and jumped into Tom's arms thrusting her little arms around his neck, "I love you, papa."

Alison and Rod were in good spirits. Rod loved company but he usually insulted them unknowingly before their visits were over. He had been grilling for hours, downing beers and pacing on the deck while they made their trip. The next-door neighbors on both sides were invited too. Tim and Erin Rodgers were there. Tim was a Fed Ex pilot and Erin a stay-at-home mom with a master's degree. Billy and Wendy Myer and their kids Townsend, Claiborne and Cathleen were just arriving. It was a good crowd. Tom was well-acquainted with them all through his many weekend visits and Molly knew them as neighbors.

After the bags were brought in and the preliminaries complete, they lounged on the deck. Candles flickered while crickets and frogs from their small lake provided a drone that became a quiet, lulling surrender. Geese, ducks and turtles drifted without a purpose into and out of the light. It was a pleasant night, clear, with a full moon and infinite star-filled sky.

Ryan held Stephanie on his lap as she laid her head on his shoulder. They were quiet and tired from the long trip. The others were gathered around the deck umbrella, sharing wine and talking. Billy had brought Pick a Peppa, cream cheese and soy sauce. Everybody commented on how such a simple idea could work so well as they nibbled away.

Alison leaned her head into Tom's shoulder and whispered, "Your book has gone to the printer."

She knew he was uncomfortable talking about *The Hung Jury*, but she also knew he was anxious. He had no idea how the process was unfolding. He left everything to her.

"It won't be long until it's available at Barnes and Noble."

He smiled, then warily asked, "Do you really think anyone will buy that book?"

"Oh, heck yes, I think you'll be a millionaire," she chirped.

Billy Myer had been dipping into the Pick a Peppa and cream cheese. Tom thought he may have been listening. Billy was the senior partner in a prestigious Hernando law firm. He had an alluring southern drawl and he oozed country charm. He was acclaimed by the neighborhood as expert on subjects ranging from constitutional law to spiritual embodiment. The neighborhood collectively would not render a decision on anything unless Billy was available for his opinion.

He had an elbow on the table; his eyes were lowered, his face expressionless. "The Killer," Jerry Lee Lewis, was represented by Billy as were many other famous people but he never gave up information. He talked about Jerry Lee in personal terms but never in legal course. His kids were allowed to perambulate wherever they chose as long as their conduct was acceptable. He set parameters for them and held them responsible, but he never hovered. As proof, a ragged-looking tree house stuck out like a sore thumb, hulking in the trees along the property line. They had dragged lumber in from every construction site in the subdivision and day by day the tree house went higher with tap, tap, tapping of their hammers until it was three shaky stories high and possibly 25 feet above ground level. Earlier in the evening Townsend and Cathleen were flying out of it like little bats and dropping into the lake below. Billy was calm about such things. Some neighbors like nervous nellies worried about bacteria in the lake and the possibility of the tree house disintegrating under their feet, but Billy simply listened, smiled, then disregarded the notion that anything serious might happen to them.

"I don't read as much as I'd like to," he said, casually joining the conversation.

"I don't read much at all anymore," Tom admitted.

"Well," Billy said, "It's a pleasure to read at any rate."

"Oh, I used to read a lot," Tom continued, "I've read all the old stuff, all Mark Twain's books and short stories, and Charles Dickens, and naturally *The Catcher in The Rye, The Great Gatsby*. I read *The Day of The Jackal, Seven Days in May, Wheels,*

Trinity, and a number of others, but I just haven't read anything lately. Not since the 80s."

"Why's that, Tom?" Billy asked, astounded that a person would deprive themselves of the pleasure. Tom just shook his head. He didn't really have an answer.

"Do you mean to tell me you haven't read John Grisham?"

"Just *A Time to Kill*, but who hasn't? But I mean I don't read on a regular basis. I read Grisham maybe three years ago. I think that was the last time I read a novel."

Billy dipped into the cream cheese and Pick a Peppa. Townsend had slipped up and now rested against Billy's side. He listened intently as the grownups talked

"You never read *The Firm*?"

"Nope, I saw the movie."

"John Grisham used my name in that book and never gave me credit," he said with a half-smile.

"You knew him?" "Yeah, I knew him. We both went to Ole Miss. He was going out when I was going in. I knew him but I don't know if he knew me."

Townsend watched his dad with admiration. It was apparent he idolized him.

"He got my dad fired," he said.

Billy turned and shot him a perturbed glance.

"I mean in the book," he quickly added.

"Yes, Billy Myer in the book was fired," he said, "But really I don't think Grisham would remember me."

They talked more about books as the candles burned lower and the moon and stars shown brighter. Ryan was talking with Tim Rodgers. Tim was explaining how he had lost the Liberty Bowl in 2000. He was the place kicker and missed a short field goal trailing by two points with no time left on the clock.

It was late but before they parted, Billy recommended a few books, naming *Marathon Man* as his favorite. Tim and Erin, Wendy and the kids were descending into the darkness, headed for their respective residences. Ryan, Stephanie and Rod were inside. Molly picked up and went inside too. Alison, Tom and Billy were left. Billy had not said a word about the conversation pertaining to *The Hung Jury*. Billy was a southern gentleman, but he was a lawyer too. Billy held his cards close to his chest. He was easy going and friendly, but Tom thought he might be different in court. The knowledge he camouflaged with charm here on the back porch might just turn into legal voodoo inside a courtroom where he would release it upon his opposition. Nonetheless, Tom liked Billy very much.

Billy stepped off the deck, waved over his head without looking back, but then he hesitated momentarily and turned around.

"A writer who writes more than he reads in not a good writer," he smiled.

Tom smiled. He thought if he ever wrote the Great American Novel Billy wouldn't have to guess if the Billy Myer therein might be himself.

Alison and Rod's house was a revolving door. Visitors from Illinois were there continually. Molly lived there and Tom was a frequent overnight guest. They had five bedrooms and it wasn't unusual for all to be occupied. On this weekend Tom, Molly, Ryan and Stephanie were there but Molly's sister and her family were also coming into town. Molly and Lana were twins. Lana's husband Don was Tom's closest friend since before they were married. Don was a senior in high school and Molly and Lana were juniors when they all started hanging around together. Don and Lana's daughter Jenny had come to Mississippi to attend Mississippi Tech. She remained there after she graduated. Now they all happened upon Mississippi and Memphis, Tennessee as they had happened upon each other in life.

As the weekend began to snowball Alison flew into action. She made an itinerary for her guests, which included an excursion to Beale St. She acquired a stretch limo and put a plan into action. All travelers arriving on Friday (Tom, Molly, Ryan and Stephanie,) would sleep in. All Saturday arrivals, which would be Don, Lana, their son, Jarod, his wife

Kari and their two kids, Isabella and Avah, would have breakfast, prepared by Tom and Don; loiter around until afternoon, have drinks and snacks on the deck and argue about ridiculous matters; then take the limo from Hernando to Memphis.

At six P.M. on Saturday, all Alison's plans had been accomplished. The sun was still hot and the air as thick as chowder. Ryan and Jarod had broken Rod's pedal-cycle leaving him in a bad mood. Tom and Don were arguing about sports. It was the baseball versus hockey comparison again. Don's claim was that baseball players are overpaid and overweight! Tom contended that hockey is a minor league sport played by toothless fuckers who couldn't make it in any other sport. That was about the whole crux of it, but it was heated. Later in the evening Don suggested that maybe they had sunken to a new low. Now they looked at each other sympathetically, knowing it was all good. They were still best friends.

A babysitter lay the children by the heels and the gang hung out the washing; as they say, they were off and underway in magnificent fashion. The limo was jam-packed and the ladies were looking fine in their little black dresses. They were already red-eyed from alcohol consumed on the deck and now into giggling fits. The female concourse was pleasantly overwhelming. Alison had completely rebounded from her weight gain with Adison. She was graceful and athletic. Kari was petite with blond hair and bright blue eyes. Stephanie was tall and elegant with thick brown hair and dark eyes. The limo driver was professional but disguising his appreciation was not without effort.

Molly might have found everything ridiculously amusing in that she wore her wry little smile and had opened up her hollow leg early. She was wearing a slim fitting black dress that hit her at her knees. The chicken wings had not influenced the way it hung, and she was stunning. She and Lana were supposed to be identical, but Molly was tall, and Lana was short. Molly wore her hair shoulder length while Lana's hair was above her ears. Molly was a classical beauty and Lana had been the cute one in school. They were both dressed to the nines and ready for Beale St. The men were dressed in casual slacks and short-sleeve shirts, looking more like a bowling team than like escorts for their counterparts, but the girls didn't seem to be bothered.

They cruised into Memphis on I-55 and slowed for traffic on Riverside Dr. Magnificent homes stood regally atop the bluff with new but meticulously groomed landscaping that cascaded the hundred-foot drop. Their enormous windows overlooked Riverside Park, situated upon the mighty Mississippi River. The limo turned onto Beale St., then onto Union. The lights from the bridge to Mud Island were simmering on the river, and the monstrous black pyramid was visible on the night sky. Yellow and red lights from Peabody Place illuminated low hanging clouds over the city. The sound of music was filtering up the alleys and into the streets. A white carriage slowly moseyed down the brick pavement with tourists hanging out the sides, snapping pictures of other tourists situated outside restaurants on wrought-iron chairs, swilling alcoholic beverages. They vacated the limo at Peabody Place crossing the street to Peabody Hotel. They wanted to see the ducks, but they had already escorted the bellhop to the elevator by the time they got there. Tom and Molly had been there several times when the ducks hopped out of the fountain and waddled to the elevator with the bellhop following them obediently, but some of the others had never seen the odd little tradition. Jimmy Buffett had even mentioned it in one of his songs.

They had wine and beer in the lobby then they had more beer at the Flying Saucer. It was comforting to know the limo was hiding away waiting for their return to Hernando. They stopped again at Alfred's for still more beer, wine and another round of eats.

Finally, they reached that one place in Memphis they agreed upon to be the second greatest bar in the world, Silky O'Sullivan's. The first being Fast Eddy's in Alton, Illinois. When they walked in the pianos were silent. The two pianos are situated on the stage back-to-back allowing the musicians to interact while playing. The small stage has space for performers but mostly the piano players do the singing and entertaining. The building is ancient with brick walls and oil floors, rustic tables and chairs and the classical lengthy bar against the opposite wall. The crowds are usually white but diverse. People from all across the country and frequently groups from Europe gather there. It's a happy place and without the sentimentality their group had for Fast Eddy's, it might just be the best bar in the world. As they filed in the door, walking past the stage, a red-haired, thin, freckle-faced man on stage took a drag off his cigarette and pointed at Rod.

"Hey, are you here with your mother-in-law again?" He grinned implying something naughty.

Molly laughed. He looked at her over his glasses, "If that's momma, I can't wait to see her daughter." Rod pointed to Alison who was leading the entourage. He dropped his cigarette and smashed it onto the floor. "Oh, yeah," he said, sitting down onto the piano bench; instantly he was pounding out a Jerry Lee rendition. The other player threw his leg over his bench and the music was on.

"Oh, yeah, you know what I like!"

Rod had taken Molly to catch a train earlier in the summer and her arriving train was broken down somewhere near New Orleans, so she canceled her trip. They spent their evening at Silky O'Sullivan's instead. The piano player couldn't resist the implication.

The songs were familiar, and the crowd was high-spirited. Silky O'Sullivan himself was there in a corner with an Elvis lookalike. Silky was in his usual dressed down attire, wearing a blue T-shirt, a white straw hat and a tan pants that looked like a house full of scumbags had just moved out of them. He looked more like he would be putting in a garden.

If an entire place; a building or an establishment can be alive and inundated with pleasure, then even the bricks in the walls were smiling. The alcohol was taking effect and the girls were "whooping," as girls do when inebriated. A good song or lively music, or even a good-looking guy on his way to the john was cause for a good "whoop."

Molly's sweet little smile was now frozen on her face. She and Lana laid off the "whoops," but they giggled like teenagers. People from Arkansas, Mississippi, Missouri and Tennessee and from everywhere gathered around their table. They talked too loudly, laughed too long and became too friendly, but in the end it was just the right amount of merriment.

Tom, Ryan and Don had their arms draped across each other spouting something patriotic, or something about family, or something they could all believe in and agree upon. Jarod leaned his back against a wall, smiled quietly as he usually did, occasionally laughing, and frequently without warning spouting, "Fuck the pedal-cycle!"

Tom watched Alison talking to a middle-aged man who had gravitated to their group. She smiled occasionally, pointing to Tom. Each time the man looked up and studied him. After their conversation he crossed the floor to Tom, holding a pen and small pad in his hand.

"Mr. Webster, I understand you're the author of *The Hung Jury*," he stated in a very British accent. Tom put his arm across the fellow's shoulder and asked him to repeat himself. The pianos were jangling, and the players were singing, entirely overwhelming attempts at conversation.

"I'd like your autograph, sir," he said sheepishly.

Tom chuckled. "Have you read *The Hung Jury*?" he asked, knowing already that it was impossible. He glowered at Alison. She was smiling widely and nodding her head in an affirmative gesture.

"Not yet, sir, but I'll be looking for it, I assure you."

Tom looked over his shoulder and saw Alison still watching him. She was 15 feet away and the music was too loud for him to scold her.

He took the pen and the little pad and signed his name with a flare then returned it to the Englishman.

"We love England," he said. "But we hate France!"

"We hate 'em too," the Englishman concurred.

Alison came to Tom's side, laughing hysterically. She kissed him on the cheek. "You're a celebrity," she giggled.

"My book hasn't even been published yet," he said, maybe too seriously for the situation, then he added lightly, "Yes, I am. I'm the next goddamn Tom Clancy." Ryan and Jarod were chuckling again about breaking Rod's pedal-cycle. Rod was pretending to be pissed off about it. Don was listening to Alison and Tom. He was befuddled. He didn't know about any book. He watched Tom, perplexed by the conversation.

"It's a long story, buddy," Tom said, smacking his pal across the back.

Alison returned to the "whooping," and Tom abandoned Don momentarily, going to the stage to make a request. He dropped a five into the galvanized bucket along with the request tag, then returned to their table.

The red-haired piano player plucked it out and read it with a disturbed expression.

"What's with you fuck'n Yankees and Brown Eyed Girl?" he shouted.

The bar went up in a roar of laughter and cheers. The Mississippians, the Missourians, the Tennesseans, Arkansans, the Englishmen and people from everywhere were with the Yankees on that song.

"Alright, but this is the last time," he shouted.

Then he started, "*Oh where did we go, now that I'm all on my own.*"

The girls were first to join in, then Ryan, and Jarod, then most of the bar followed suit. Tom had never sung a word aloud in his life but just then his mouth opened, and words began to form.

"*All along the water falls with you, my brown eyed girl, fa, la, la, la, la, la, la, la, la, de, da, just like that.*"

Molly watched him. Her smile was wider, and her eyes were fixed on him. She marveled at his total inability to carry a tune. She laughed affectionately, then came to his side and put her arms around his waist. Don wrapped his arm across his shoulder, Ryan and Jarod joined in, then the girls and Lana, then the Mississippians, Missourians,

Tennesseans, the people from everywhere and England were circling around holding each other, singing louder than they had ever sung, swaying together until their voices not quite harmonizing but fused together into the most extraordinary song ever heard. The piano players stopped playing and gaped in disbelief. The crowd clapped their hands in unison carrying the song for five minutes while the piano players smoked.

After allowing the revelers to slow, they struck up a different tune, a quiet, safe tune and the hordes returned to their tables. Molly hung onto Tom's arm as he went to the bar to retrieve his credit card. He nearly swallowed his glass when he discovered his tab was $468.00. He paid it thinking it was a lesson well learned, but still he would have done it again. The group agreed upon one last drink. That slower, quieter, closing time music hovered over their table and slid down the walls and kissed up against the windows and finally floated across the floor and bumped into the exit. Tom went to the galvanized bucket and spoke to his red-haired, freckled -aced piano playing friend. He dropped a 20 into the bucket.

"I've got a 20-dollar request here for a song. He wants me to play something of my choosing – something I really love."

They walked up Beale St. as young kids back flipped endlessly down the street while people cheered. They could hear a soft sweet song coming from Silky O'Sullivan's. It was a song they had never heard before, but it was a song about the South.

Chapter V

On Sunday morning hangovers prevailed. The sun bore down unmercifully; sweat was being mopped off foreheads and necks, while limp hair gathered moisture from the air. Those who had dragged themselves out of bed before 10 sat motionlessly on the deck. The air conditioner system had revolted at some point during the night and now they sat stewing in the humidity.

Billy was standing in his yard watching his kids swimming in the lake. Townsend, Claiborne and Cathleen were in with only their heads poking out of the water. Tom thought they resembled little sea lions quietly watching the activity, or the lack of it, on the deck. Billy was having coffee. Tom joined him at the property line.

It was already 10:30. "Did you know the limo driver is asleep in the driveway out front?" Billy asked.

"I wouldn't doubt it. We were out all night," Tom laughed.

"No – he really is," Billy assured.

Tom glanced around the corner and observed the long black car in the driveway. "I'll be right back," he said.

He walked around to the limo and pecked on the driver's window. A young black man stepped out. He was a little rumpled but still somewhat presentable. Tom took the driver's business card and opened his wallet. He tipped the driver then looked back to Billy. He glanced at the business card. It said Downtown Limo Service, St. Louis/Memphis. The driver said, "It's my grandpa's company. We're trying to expand into the Memphis area." Tom recognized the name. He had heard it advertised on KMOX Radio in St. Louis.

Billy was still watching. Tom took all the bills he had in his wallet and held them in the air and shook them like they were trying to fly away. They both laughed.

When he rejoined Billy, he wore a serious expression. "You know, I was thinking about your comment, Tom. You know the one about where are all the poor people." Billy said.

"It's true," Tom argued. "You always hear about all the poor people in Mississippi and the poverty. I just don't see it."

"It's here. You're just looking in all the wrong places."

"There are poor people everywhere," Tom argued. He knew there were rural areas in Illinois filled with people who live in shacks surrounded by junk cars, with goats, chickens and hordes of dogs running loose on their properties.

Tom pointed to Billy's house. It was a 400,000-dollar home. In Chicago it would sell for more than a million. Northerners wouldn't be able to relate to owning a property like that for that price.

Being modest Billy said, "Big house, big mortgage." He was embarrassed by his success and wealth.

"Tom, we're gonna take a trip one of these weekends and I'll show you some real poverty. We'll go all down through the Delta. Molly can drive, I'll navigate and you man the cooler in the back seat. We'll see some poor people."

Tom agreed, "We'll call it the Delta trip. I'll look forward to it."

With that they parted, and preparations were made for Tom, Molly, Ryan and Stephanie's departure. They had their own adventure ahead of them.

They retraced their Friday trek going north on I-55 from Memphis through Arkansas, through Cape Girardeau, Missouri, then Perryville and on to St. Mary's Landing.

When they came to the sawmill, they saw several cars parked along the road and in the pasture beside the sawmill park pavilion. There were 40 to 50 people and as many horses and mules prancing about, and party-like activity was everywhere. Glen and Joe were hosting a law enforcement charity ride. The state police and local police officers were joined together in their annual ride for kids.

The property belonged to Glen and Joe and in addition to the park pavilion they had a fishing pond and riding stables. They had built the park for entertainment for the Webster family, but it had become a community recreational facility by proxy.

Glen was grilling and Joe was leading the ride. Tom had forgotten about the event but was eager to join. Molly believed he never got enough. He was a last dog even now at sixty. She looked at him sideways, then shrugged her shoulders. They would have no choice but to join in. She and Ryan grabbed a ride. Ryan got Glen's black stallion and Molly was assigned to Joe's gentle little mule, Old Kate. Tom stayed behind to talk with Glen. When Molly rode by them, she scowled, bit her lower lip and her eyes burned into Tom, daring him to so much as smile. How could they put her on a little brown mule! Stephanie went to the mill office to lie down.

When they were gone Tom and Glen were alone. At the first opportunity Glen asked how Molly was taking their little trip. He had no idea Tom was anxious to do some research.

"She gets a little distressed talking about all the fights we've had."

"What do you mean? We didn't talk about fights."

"Well, I told her about Pop batting Gilbert's head."

They both laughed.

"I still haven't told her about him shooting that guy."

They laughed again.

It was another fiasco Pop had been in. There were no newspaper articles to rely on, or eyewitnesses to confer with, just Pop's version of a gun fight he had survived.

Tom became serious for a moment. "You know, I'm not real clear on how that all went down," he said. "I mean I know what Pop told me about it, but I was only nine or ten. Now Ryan wants details and I'd like to get it right."

"Why don't you tell me what Pop said and I'll fill in the blanks?" Glen said.

"Pop said Harold, (his younger brother,) had been chasing this guy's wife. Harold wasn't married and the woman wasn't a bastion of morality, so they got the deal done, you know what I mean." Tom said.

Glen laughed at his description.

"Well Pop and Harold looked so much alike that this guy thought Pop was the one who was messing around with her. He had been spouting all around the county that he was laying for Pop and not

Harold. Pop heard all this, so he was keeping his eye peeled for the man. One afternoon Pop was headed home when he saw a truck stopped ahead. He knew it was that guy's truck. He stopped and put his gearshift into low and got out to walk alongside the truck. He had the door swung open for protection. As he crept along, he reached inside the truck and got his shotgun from the rack. He could see the guy up ahead with a rifle. The man took aim at him and fired, just grazing his ear. He stayed hunched down still keeping up with the truck as it idled down the road. When he got within range he stepped out and fired a shot hitting the man in the chest."

Glen sighed in disbelief. "That ain't right, but go on."

"That's what he told me." Tom chuckled.

"Go on, finish it."

"He ran home, and he started furiously packing his clothes. Grandpa Webster came in and wanted to know what he was doing. Pop and Mom lived with Grandpa and Grandma at the time. Pop told him he had shot a man. After Grandpa got the story he said, "Hell, boy, that's self-defense!""

Glen rolled his eyes then looked at the floor. He laughed quietly for a moment. "Do you know what part of that is true?"

Tom stopped and thought for an instant. "None of it," he said sheepishly.

"No, there was one thing true. He shot the man in the chest. Everything else is bullshit. I know because I helped pick the glass out of his back."

Now Tom was bewildered. "What glass?"

"He had glass fragments in his back! He wasn't shot!" Glen belly laughed.

"Now I'll tell you what really happened," Glen said. "Pop was down on Current River gigging fish with a three-pronged gig. This man and his wife lived up the river a-ways from where he had his boat tied up. They saw him down there and struck up a conversation. They all went up to the house and had coffee and talked. They got on pretty well, and when Pop left everything was "hunky dorrie;" they were buddies, you might say. A few days later Pop went back when the woman was there alone. I can't say what happened but whatever it was, the old boy didn't like it much. He saw where Pop's gig had left marks in the mud outside the back door – evidence, you might say. He put two and two together and he didn't like the way it added up. He was laying for Pop to come back for another round with his wife, and Pop did. That's when the heat was turned up. When Pop got out of the truck the old boy came out toting a rifle. Pop seen him taking aim and he run for the truck. Just when he got in, the old boy shot out the back window. The glass buried in his back and arms. Pop grabbed his shotgun and plugged him in the chest. He went down like a bag of spuds. Pop took off like a bat out a hell. He went home and got Grandpa and they drove back out there. They thought they would find him dead in the yard, but he was gone. Grandpa went up to the house and found the man getting patched up. He was buggered up but he wasn't in danger of dying. He told Grandpa that the valley wasn't big enough for both of 'em and a few days later he was gone. They didn't even call the Sheriff."

"That's crazy," Tom said, smiling half-heartedly.

"That's the truth," Glen said. "How old were you when he told you that story?"

"Nine, maybe ten."

"Well, I guess he couldn't tell you the truth," Glen said with a chuckle.

"What about mom?"

"She wasn't happy. There was a little bit of tension around there for a while." A small laugh followed.

They sat silently for a few minutes. Glen turned the meat and sprinkled water on the charcoal. It sizzled and smoke puffed upward.

"That's the truth," Glen said in a reinforcing way.

"That's crazy. All this time I thought he was some kind of hero defending himself, facing down a deranged jilted lover!" Another long pause followed.

"So that's the true story?" Tom chuckled. Glen started laughing too. A perplexed but amused expression was plastered on their faces. In a few moments, tears were flowing down Tom's cheek as he tried to talk through his laughter. Finally he spluttered, "what a farce!"

Soon the trail ride was over. The meat was done, and the riders gathered for the cookout and festivities that followed. Ryan and Molly were clamoring about their respective rides. Molly had forgiven Old Kate for being a mule and had acquired affection for her. Ryan walked with his arm over her shoulder and it was apparent they had been enlivened by their participation in the event.

The sun was beginning to set, and an orange glow glistened above the tree line. Fireflies blinked in the shadows while frogs and crickets clamored. It had been a long day. The revelers were popping beers and a guitar player was strumming, but Tom, Molly, Ryan and Stephanie were expended from the trail ride and Beale Street excesses.

When Molly and Tom talked, Tom didn't mention his conversation with Glen. He just said he had fun. Sometimes the best story is the one you can't repeat.

"Is this what you expected?" she asked, knowing it wasn't but she was curious about his considerations.

"No, but I'm having fun and we have three more days."

They called for two rooms at Freda's Motel at exit 133 on I-55 which was completely unnecessary. If that motel was full there surely were many desperate travelers on the road. It was a dump, but convenient. Ryan and Stephanie were going to return to Milwaukee on Monday, while Tom and Molly would go on alone. Ryan was a workaholic and couldn't be away from his office for more than a day without being in a fit. He had already taken 15 calls and handled several matters by phone. Molly called Hertz to have a car delivered to the hotel on Monday morning. Now they just needed to get to their rooms and settle in.

Before leaving St. Mary's Landing they stopped at Junior's Tap for a bottle of wine. Molly was ready to talk about their day before retiring, and a glass of wine in the room was an appealing prospect. Junior's was the only building occupying the east side of Main St., but the cracked sidewalks and the crumbling facade was signaling the end for that place too. Tom and Molly left Ryan and Stephanie to go inside. When they entered, the old familiar odors jolted Tom's senses. It was that distinctive old dive smell. The shuffleboard, the juke box and the bar lights were all there gleaming yellow and red and green, but still leaving the place dim and dismal. An excessively large man behind the bar smiled. It was Junior Gilmer. He was Glen's age and Tom had known him all his life. There was one lone customer sitting with his hands wrapped around a beer bottle.

"Hey, Tommy, doin' the down-home thang?" Junior asked cheerfully.

"Just passing through, Junior. We're headed for Freda's. We just need a couple bottles of wine."

"We've got 'er, buddy. How many ya need?"

"Anything will do, maybe a bottle of zinfandel, and a chardonnay."

"Huh," he spoke in disbelief as he screwed an expression upon his features as though he had been asked the most stupid question he ever heard.

"I got strawberry or apple'" he stated flatly.

Molly gawked at him in disbelief.

"What kind?" she asked.

"Strawberry or apple," he said again.

"I mean what winery?"

Junior drew his chin in, pulled his glasses down on his nose and scrutinized her.

"Boone's Farm," he spouted.

"I'm not drinking Boone's Farm," she said defiantly.

"Suit yourself then!" he said, turning his back on her to pick up a bar towel.

Tom laughed. It took less time for them to garner a dislike for each other than it took Neil Armstrong to take one giant leap for mankind.

"Do you mean to tell me with Crown Valley and Chaumette wineries less than 20 miles from here you have to sell Boone's Farm?"

"That's all my customers want. They don't want no Crown Valley kerosene. They want something light and tasty. They want Boone's Farm. God dammit!"

Tom decided maybe they would settle for Millers Chill. Junior wasn't sure he had that either, but he volunteered to check the walk-in for it. As he went by he shot Molly a dirty look.

Tom studied the lone customer and he realized it was Darrell Fox, a boy now grown to be a shriveled up little old man.

"Hey, Foxy, how ya doing!"

Foxy looked up through bloodshot eyes.

"How do you think I'm doing? It's Sunday evening and I'm drunk. I've been drunk all day," he said with obvious irritation.

Junior was back with a green cardboard package. He had found the Chill.

"I got'er Tommy," he said slapping the box with a chubby hand.

"Foxy, remember me, Tom Webster?"

"Yea, I remember you, Mr. Tom Webster," he replied curtly.

Tom glanced at Junior, hoping for an explanation.

"He's got a hard on for Glen, Tommy. Glen loaned him money he won't pay back, and now Glen's the asshole. I guess all you Websters are, huh, Foxy."

"Wasn't that you getting out of that big black SUV, Mr. Tom Webster?" Foxy smirked.

Tom didn't reply.

"Big fuck'n car!"

"It's a Dodge, Foxy."

"Oh! Just a big fancy new Dodge ain't good enough for Mr. Tom Webster!" He said, turning back to his drink and mumbling other inaudible remarks.

Junior was amused. He could see that Tom was totally confounded by Foxy's attitude.

"Last time I seen you, Tommy, you was driving a Lexus 500."

"That's Molly's car. I drive a Hyundai," Tom said, somewhat perturbed. Molly saw his eyes and knew it was time to move in.

"Let's go," she said quietly.

Foxy un-wrapped his hand from his bottle and turned on his bar stool and stared at Tom through bloodshot eyes.

"You fuck'n Websters got it made, don't you!"

Tom remained silent as Molly tugged on his arm. Foxy was too drunk to be taken seriously but his crap was starting to hit home.

"You know I done everything right and what have I got. I wanted to go to college."

"You'd a flunked out," Junior chimed in.

"I wanted to go to college, but Dad was sick with TB, and I stayed home and took over the hardware store. And now look at me! The fuck'n Walmart, and the fuck'n Lowe's and the fuck'n Menards! And you, you done everything wrong. You fought the teachers and everybody else in school. You were a state policeman and you worked for the governor's office. How'd you pull that off being a high school drop out! Hell, I heard you own a technical college in Memphis. I worked hard and done everything right and now I'm broke and a drunk. You took the easy way out and look at you!"

"Fuck you Foxy, we were the poorest family in this town!"

Molly pulled at his elbow. "Come on, let's go," she demanded.

Tom walked to the end of the bar near the rear door. He placed a $10.00 bill down.

"Get Foxy another round, Junior."

"Hell, that'll get him ten of them draught beers."

"Keep the change then Junior. Haven't you heard I'm rich!"

"You come back when you're in town, Tommy. I'll be here unless Foxy's run off all my business, and I have to close my doors."

When they were back in the car Tom was steaming. "Fucking loser," he snorted. Molly rolled her eyes.

"State Police, where'd he get that shit? The Governor's Office, Jesus Christ!"

Molly shot him an irritated look. "You're mad that he got his facts wrong. You were slapping him on the back just five minutes ago."

"Hey, I never said a goddamn thing to him."

Ryan and Stephanie sat silently trying to catch up without asking.

"You didn't have to stand there and listen."

"Whatever," Tom said, ending the quarrel.

Ryan was driving and Stephanie was making polite remarks but failing to get a conversation started. She was nervous. She had never seen them argue before.

They sat quietly in the back seat. Tom's mind churned mulling over Foxy's remarks. He was a high school dropout, and a liar. He couldn't deny it, but in his own defense he took the GED test without attending even one class and he graduated from college, although it had been somewhat out of sequence.

"I graduated first in my class," he muttered.

"What, Dad?" Ryan asked.

"Nothing son, just talking to myself."

Molly looked out one window and Tom the other. Tom thought about his life, and his poverty. He knew poverty better than anyone. Many people don't know anything about being poor. They see video of the ghettos with people walking around in Starter jackets and wearing 200-dollar shoes and they still call it poverty. There wasn't a hundred dollars' worth of shoes on his entire family when they were in the throes of poverty. Foxy's ignorance was galling. Tom wanted Foxy to know what a life he had lived. He wanted him to know he had lived in a house with dirt floors, and on an abandoned houseboat, and in a dance hall with no running water or electricity or heat. He wanted him to know how hard it was to do homework when there wasn't a place where you could study without distractions or where it was warm enough or where there was adequate lighting to read the print. He just wanted the son-of-a-bitch to know it wasn't that easy.

The houseboat was only a vague memory, but the dance hall was vividly imprinted in his mind. It was a concrete structure two and a half stories tall. It was empty, lacking inner walls, cabinets, heating, running water or any other facility resembling civilized accommodations. They called it the old dike. He never knew why or from where the name came. His dad and Glen installed a cook stove and a wood-burning heating stove. The cook stove came from behind a neighbor's shed. He didn't recall a purchase and knew by the fact they couldn't buy a pound of bologna that they didn't pay for it. It was either given to them or they borrowed it, in a manner of speaking.

The cook stove was heavy steel with ceramic doors and a hood over the top where food was left to warm. It was a fabulous stove and today it would be worth a fortune. The heating stove was a cheap round barrel like piece of tin, maybe an eighth of an inch thick. Those stoves were available in any variety store or hardware store anywhere. Foxy's dad undoubtedly sold hundreds. It's likely that many hillbilly homes went up in flames as a result. Willy would fill that thing with lumber scraps from the sawmill, light it up and the sides would glow red. Sometimes it was so hot that the stovepipe would glow all the way to the chimney. Tom had seen that stove literally walking because it was so hot, just giggling around, staying put only because it was attached to the stovepipe. Usually after one season the stove would have holes in the sides and occasionally hot embers would drop out onto the floor. Still Tom recalled they all huddled around that stove and talked and laughed like fools.

Willy and Glen brought lumber from the mill and built walls on the first level. The ceilings were probably 20 feet high. It was a monstrous building totally not designed for family dwelling. The only lumber available was green (uncured) cottonwood, suitable for pallets and crates but never for construction. If cottonwood is left outside in the weather, it will rot and disintegrate rapidly. It's more sap than wood and when it dries it shrinks considerably. When the job was finished, they had large bedrooms and a spacious living room and kitchen. Tom recalled being happy and proud. After three weeks the lumber began to dry and there were spaces between the boards two inches wide. You knew who was whistling anywhere in the house. All those little eyes looking through the cracks crushed all hopes of privacy.

It was so cold that winter, Tom thought he would never be warm again. The old dike had no insulation and the massive building could not be heated with a small heating stove and a cook stove. They all hovered around their tin bellied stove, glowing red hot with embers falling out onto the floor. Their knees were burning while their backsides froze. They held their jeans away from their skin to avoid the sting and laughed away the hours totally oblivious to their condition. They were surviving but it wasn't exactly the easy route.

"Dim your lights, asshole," Ryan spouted, snapping Tom back to the present.

He eyed Molly sideways, not wanting her to know but hoping she would soften. She reached across the seat and placed her hand on his thigh. "It's okay," she said.

He smiled. It was, in fact, okay.

Monday morning brought cooler weather. Ryan and Stephanie headed for Milwaukee, commenting that a short stop at Laclede's Landing might be in order. Ryan hugged them both and said "I love you" as he had done every day of his life. He was a good son.

Chapter VI

Tom and Molly were off to locations vague in Tom's memory or places he had heard about from others. When an adult recalls pleasant childhood memories, the memory doesn't fit reality. This was certainly the case for him. Tom's inclination was to live those days in only the best terms, recalling the best: not including the bitter truth, but only the comforting aspects of those bygone years. Even the memory of the old dike couldn't sully his perceptions. Tom and Molly often laughed about his advocating spinach, spam and Vienna sausages, truly delicacies from those hard times, but when they were put upon the table he found them to be obnoxious. His defense was that they clearly didn't have the same ingredients as they had in those days.

Tom and Molly were not a Tom and a Molly. They had been together so long and so close that they were Tom'n'Molly. They were an entity unto themselves, a pair, not two individuals. They did not agree on everything or press forward like a barge loaded with grain headed down the Mississippi River, but together like a dust devil stirring across an open field: a torrent with pieces flying in different directions, swirling, pitching upward,, downward and across but holding together, flying past highways, open ground and trees and maintaining momentum headed to a common destination.

Molly didn't believe this exploration was worth the effort. This story, this ultimate in violence and civil discourse was distasteful to her, but she would follow along in the center as the debris gathered and fell and hit upon obstacles along the way. It was simple to her; the story was too old to be accurate and not worthy in the end to be revisited, but still she saddled up and headed off into the horizon.

They drove south on highway N through the hills where the roads curved snakelike across rivers and valleys and narrow bridges past hazardous intersections laden with faded silk flowers. Tom was not naïve or some floundering incompetent idiot driving mindlessly across land masses merely asking dumb questions along the way. He still used a typewriter and not the laptop Molly gave him, but he was knowledgeable in the technology required to be a good investigator. He had employees whom he assigned to research on the internet and other services available to him and his agency for finding facts and information. They had found nothing, but he knew the best results are found firsthand and on the ground. And in reality, this was not an investigation. There would be no evidence for trial, no evidence hearing or cross examination to determine his sources or his judgment. It would be submitted only to his scrutiny, but still in the end he wanted it to be revealing and honest.

There was a photograph of Lawrence Black and Addy Black standing in front of the Van Buren County Courthouse. They lived in Fremont, which was a short drive from there. By their appearance they were in their late 30s or early 40s. This would have put him within the age required to fit the puzzle, so Van Buren was where they would start.

Those old black and white photos tucked away in boxes and pushed back inside obscure drawers don't reveal the true character or value of the people represented therein. Would we be so proud of them if they came to life, dirty, greasy, and unkempt, leaving a stink trail as they rambled about without an ounce of gumption or dignity? Sometimes those people in photographs were not pure and pious in life, and sometimes their status was elevated in death by our perceptions. Would we want to introduce them to our friends? Are some things better left unknown, left to those haunting pictures where they are solemnly gazing into the camera lens with fixed mysterious eyes? Tom wanted to believe there was bravery, and honor, lurking within the negatives, and he wanted it to come out into the road and stand against the houses, and to walk in the streets. He wanted them to hold those grim poses until the picture was snapped but then to laugh and slap each other on the back and talk about how they might look when the film was developed. He wanted them to be people he could admire and respect. He wanted Lawrence Black to be the man his mother had described, a man who was fearless and strong but kind and gentle. He wanted him to be a man who would stand up for those he loved. He would press on with those ideals as his compass.

They drove through Farmington, Doe Run, Ironton and then south to Van Buren.

Van Buren is the county seat and is tucked away within the rocks and hills perched upon the banks of the Current River. When they crossed the bridge, the sunlight was glistening on the crystal-clear water below. The yellow gravel looked like gold, bright and gleaming deep on the river bottom. Cottonwood tufts drifted on the breeze and floated away from the car windshield as they wheeled into town. The population sign was faded but still legible. There were 918 people living there. A few cars were present on the streets, moving at a pace revealing little haste in getting to their destinations. A rusty tractor with iron wheels sat in a weed-laden lot, and the narrow streets were lined with buildings with recessed doors, wide bay windows adorned with macramé hanging planters, and advertisements from bygone years. A washed-out Santa Claus taking a sip of Coca Cola sprawled across an ancient rusty sign and an ad for Sunbeam Bread with a yellow-haired girl in pigtails was faded by time. The sidewalks were elevated and revealed traces of numerous repairs from antiquity. Tom had been here when he was a child and it didn't seem to have changed. It was a museum of small-town life.

They found the small courthouse and were soon standing, just looking at it in a puzzled sort of way. One entrance was indistinguishable from the other. It was the same on all four sides. Tom wanted to know the exact location where his grandparents were when the picture was taken, but it really didn't matter. Tom looked at the streets, buildings, the shops and trees. The street signs were rusty, and the names obliterated.

Tom started walking across the street.

"Where are you going?" Molly asked.

"To the Post Office."

Molly laughed, "So that's how you do an investigation!"

"Yes, that's where you start."

"I expected something more elaborate than that."

"I'm an interrogator, that's what I do best. I let the boys bring 'em in and I do the talking."

"How many years has it been since you did that?" Molly smirked.

"A few," he said.

A Long Road to Redemption

They saw Old Glory waving in the breeze above a small brick building. A small metal sign said, "US Post Office – General Delivery – 1937 - Franklin Roosevelt President.

When they entered the lobby a bell over the door jingled. Molly glanced up and rolled her eyes

"We're uptown now," she said.

Mailboxes lined each wall and there was a small counter with a frosted slide window. A sign read closed for lunch. A heavy-set middle-aged woman was mopping the floor.

"Good morning," she said with a mouse-like squeaky voice. "The post office window is closed until noon."

"Great," Tom said glancing at his watch.

She shrugged her shoulders.

"Do you know any Blacks around here?" He asked.

"There's a black family down by the intersection coming into town. I know one of the sons is married to a white girl and I hear people talk but I haven't seen them."

"No, I mean Blacks with a capital B."

She looked at him puzzled by his remark, her chubby face completely blank.

"Oh, no, for God's sake, I'm stupid!"

Tom laughed politely.

"No, I don't know any Blacks. I'm not from here. I drive in from Fredericktown. I know some Flacks over at Fredericktown, but no Blacks. I know some Stacks who live here, but no Blacks." Obviously, she ran out of rhyming names, so she stopped and shrugged.

Molly watched Tom's face as he stared at the woman as though he were looking at a pile of cow manure. She wanted to laugh but refrained. Tom glanced at his watch again. The postmaster should be there soon, he thought. He tried not to look at the woman again, afraid of what his features might reveal.

"How about a newspaper. Is there a newspaper here in town?"

"I really don't know for sure. I think there was a newspaper here," she chirped. "But like I said, I drive in from Fredericktown. They got a newspaper in Fredericktown."

Tom looked at his watch again. It was ten until 12. He bit his lip to suppress his frustration. The fat woman wrung out her mop and picked up her bucket. She breathed heavily as she gasped air with her mouth wide open. She sighed and wheezed and coughed as she maneuvered her bucket and mop towards the utility room doorway. The clock on the wall read 12:00 noon. Tom looked at the window hoping the Postmaster would materialize.

"Whew, that's hard work. I'm sure glad I don't have to do that every day," the woman said. She then disappeared inside the utility doorway. After a short silence the mail room window opened. The fat mop lady stood prominently in the window. Tom turned quickly to face her.

"Oh, I thought the Postmaster was here," he said.

"She is," she jingled.

Molly's smile broadened and a short gasp escaped her lips.

"You're the Postmaster?" Tom asked indignantly.

"Yes, and the Custodian." She said.

He looked like someone had asked him to pull their finger, and not knowing the results, he pulled.

Without a word he walked outside. Molly followed him quietly chuckling as she went. She was amused at his irritability. Nowadays he tried to subdue his anger. He would often say, "Nobody loves an angry old man," but he couldn't hide it. When he was 25 he would have lit into her for her stupidity and then later bemoaned his loss of control. Now he just burned inside and bit his tongue.

They looked again up and down the street eyeballing any establishment where information might be found. Just then a battered old Ford stopped and a young man with a mail bag sprang from it. Tom intercepted him as he headed for the post office.

"Sir, I'm looking for information about an incident, I'm sure it was here in this county, and it happened a long time ago." He said.

"What would that be, sir? I was born and raised here, and I know about every gossip there is. I'm the rural mail carrier," he said, then paused. "I've been bitten by every dog in the county too, so I guess I'm qualified," he laughed.

"My grandfather was involved in an incident way back in the 30s, a gun incident. We were trying to find out more about it, but 70 years, well that's a long time ago." In that split second Tom pondered his own common sense, his voice issuing such an inane question. Would this man think he was a total idiot? His self-doubt was in full bloom. In that same moment his answer came from within. His mother had cried about something she thought her father did. There were conditions that existed in her life that were enormously painful but she stood strong, never bending and for her to cry over a memory - well, that information was worth pursuing. He wanted to know, and he would endure a little embarrassment to find answers.

"I really don't know about anything that far back, but I've heard stories about a gunfight outside

Fremont where a bunch of hillbillies shot it out. I can't give you any details though."

"Was there a Black – a Lawrence Black involved?"

"I can't say, it was just talk – tavern talk and barber shop talk. Stuff you hear but never know whether it's a bunch of bologna or not."

"Maybe there's a local newspaper."

"No. Just the shopper. It's got ads and sales, but no real news."

Molly was anxious to move on. She was already worn thin on the dead man incident.

"There is a guy who might know something. He's a famous writer, Edwin Wilhelm. He's crazy, but he gets mail from everywhere by the wheelbarrow-load. I carry books and magazines into his house by the bushel baskets. I hate the old bastard. I take stuff up there from Chicago and New York, the West Coast, and Europe too. I don't know how anybody could read all that crap."

Tom recognized the name. Edwin Wilhelm was world-renowned. He had five best sellers in the 50s and several other popular books during the 40s.

"He's a grouchy old bastard," he added. "They say he's been here since the 60s, or 50s. With all the books, newspapers and magazines he gets if anyone here knows about an article, he would."

Tom and Molly drove to out into the country. They meandered along a one lane blacktop road where barbed wire fences, cedar trees and wildflowers crowded against the pavement. They were plowing along in the same direction but certainly their notions were not on the same page. Molly could not comprehend why he would want to do this. It's easy to lose yourself in desire for fame or pursuit of riches and even to become self-deluded for the same reasons, but Molly didn't believe Tom was forged in that vein. She was trying to stay the course, but she was not a patient person and she did not suffer fits of fancy lightly. The trip had been at her suggestion, but she thought they had more pressing matters. She was living in Hernando and he was in Willoughby Hills. That condition was intolerable to her. Until the moment she laid her head on her pillow in Hernando on April 10th, 2005 she had not slept in a bed without Tom at her side for over 37 years. They were together every weekend at their cabin in Graniteville, Missouri, where Tom had built the cabin, every stick and stone, but she was uncomfortable with that situation. She just wanted him to find something in the South. She thought he could teach law enforcement classes at a junior college, or work with their investment group, or anything, just anything to be together. She thought he might be fearing old age, that maybe he was looking beyond the horizon to a future when he would not be the vital person he had been, strong and sturdy and forward thinking. This infatuation with the past was starting to concern her. Did he want to relive or rewrite history? She knew he was ashamed he had quit school, and even more ashamed he had lied to get on the police department but there was no rewrite for those things. They were written in stone. No heroics could change anything; it was as it was.

They watched for the address the route carrier had given them, finally finding a mailbox with faded characters spelling out Edwin Wilhelm. Tom didn't know how to approach someone with so much fame and success. Would he be an arrogant self-indulgent bastard who had built monuments here in the wilderness to himself? His curiosity was soon relieved as they prodded along the long lane negotiating the washed-out gullies in the deteriorating access. They found a small brick house facing the roadway. A crumbling rock wall surrounded the home as flowers, blackberry bushes and horse weeds were having rein over everything. Wild vines climbed the wall and encompassed the trees and smothered the yard, butted against the house and mounted the walls to the rooftop. There were two fountains abandoned and filled with trash blown in from the road.

Tom and Molly were doubtful, believing they had wandered into the wrong lane or had been led astray by the route carrier. Molly appeared disgusted. Tom looked at her for a signal as to what might have happened, but she was without a thought.

"Could we possibly be in the right place?" Tom muttered almost to himself.

"Edwin Wilhelm is a best seller, isn't he?"

"He was," Molly said.

"My god, I can't believe this!

They both started for the house, but Molly slowed to a saunter observing the entanglement and disarray. Tom went on to the door.

"What would a successful writer be doing here?"

Tom knocked then waited. The sun was lowering in the sky. He looked nervously at his watch. It was 7:30 p.m. This day would soon be history. While he waited, he looked across the blacktop and noticed a pathway leading to a small cemetery.

He knocked again and the door finally creaked open. There in the doorway stood an elderly man wearing a long robe with a large letter W prominently displayed on his chest. He had thick gray straw-like hair and dark skin and piercing blue eyes. He leaned on a crooked knobby cane and glared out with disdain. He looked like Moses about to part the Red Sea. He was frail and cold looking and in need of a barber.

"I'm not giving interviews!" He snapped.

"I'm not here for that," Tom said, realizing by his remark that he had the right man.

"Then what!" he snapped again.

"I'm looking for information. I'm sorry to impose, but I've heard you have knowledge of many things," he said sounding like he had just happened upon Solomon.

The old man laughed, "Knowledge, information, ha, that's all bullshit."

"I'm sorry, that was stupid. I'm just trying to find an old newspaper article. I don't know where it was printed or when. The route carrier said you were very informed about most things related to the printed word."

"That's easy stuff nowadays," he said with a smirk. "Computer stuff."

"Yes, it is, but we've done our research. There's nothing there. Now I'm legging it out."

"You're not a newspaper man, or TV?"

"No."

"Not a government agent?"

"No, just a guy."

"Just a man bumbling around going up to people you don't know like an idiot then? Is that right, boy?" he asked, stone-faced.

Tom was immediately astonished, but amused. He was sixty years old. It had been a long time since he had been called "boy." They stood silently looking at each other.

Did Wilhelm expect an answer? He continued to watch Tom's face. He did in fact expect an answer.

"Well, I don't know, but yes I guess that's right," he chuckled. After all it was an accurate statement.

"Well, come in then, boy, since you're not a government agent or newspaper man, but just a bumbling idiot asking asinine questions. I guess you're harmless enough."

Tom hesitated. He wasn't angry but suddenly he felt put upon. The old man's eyes softened a bit.

"Come on in, boy. You've come all the way out here, you might as well indulge on old man's indifference to your expectations."

As they entered Tom's eyes needed a moment to adjust to the shadowy interior. In a moment he was dumbfounded. Wilhelm shuffled navigating his way through canals of books, newspapers and magazines four feet high. The walls were lined to the ceilings and every cranny was stuffed with reading material. Mold and fungus lingered in the air and permeated the entire place. His feet scooted along the floor slowly, occasionally pausing to pick up a book or article or to peruse something quickly then to resume his journey through the maze. Finally, they came to an opening where a four-foot long table and one lone chair occupied an enclave. Walls of newspapers surrounded them. Tom stared at a computer screen in disbelief. As feeble as Wilhelm was, he was up to speed on the web. There was a screensaver of a jackass with its tail arched in the air.

"Now what is the knowledge that you seek?" Wilhelm said, mocking Tom's earlier question.

Tom was certain he wanted to ask many questions now. The conditions here had piqued his interest. It was baffling. He began with his interest in the newspaper article. Awkwardly he narrated, laying out his intentions, but leaving out the part about his writing the Great American Novel. When he finished, he waited for Wilhelm to commit an answer. Wilhelm stumbled around knocking books off their randomly assigned locations, cursing under his breath as he feebly went about boiling some water on the stove, presumably for tea. Tom thought Wilhelm might have totally forgotten he was there as he negotiated the small space. There was a pathway to a bay window facing the cemetery. At first glance the window appeared to have no glass, but after further study Tom could see that the glass was squeaky clean without even a smudge. It was oddly out of place.

Outside the window Molly was occupying her time surveying the tangled premises.

"Why do you come to me?" Wilhelm asked, turning slowly to Tom.

"It's just that they said you have a lot of newspapers and books and stuff like that. That you read incessantly."

"It has nothing to do with me being a writer? A best-selling writer? It's odd that you wouldn't mention that, boy. Why wouldn't you mention that? You were born in this country, weren't you?"

"To be honest with you I had no idea you were here. I've read your books; I mean, who hasn't? But no sir, I didn't know. When I got here I even thou…." He stopped mid-sentence realizing he was about to unintentionally disparage the untidy surroundings.

"You saw my house and you couldn't believe I live here, right?" He muttered in a quiet voice.

"I try not to assume anything."

"But it's not what you expected. Would that be accurate?"

He turned to his stove. The teapot was whistling. Tom was relieved he wouldn't have to answer the question. Wilhelm feebly reached up to a cabinet. He repositioned several paperback books in order to fetch two teacups.

Tom glanced around, looking as far as he could into the adjacent rooms. They were all the same, books and papers stacked from wall to wall covering all the floors with narrow causeways strategically angling through from point to point. It was a rat's maze.

Tom's eyes had adjusted to the darkness now and he saw a book lying at the opposite end of the table. He strained to read the title. The cover was a lighted courthouse with a blackened sky. He saw the bold print, *The Hung Jury*. His first instinct was to lunge for it, open it and verify the interior. He shot Wilhelm a puzzled glance. Wilhelm's eyes were fixed on him. He wore a small vague smile. It was a knowing smile. Tom chose not to comment. His book couldn't have come this far already, but he wondered if someone else had a copyright on his title?

Wilhelm placed the two teacups on the table and with shaky hands he poured water over the teabags.

"Why do old people always have tea?" He paused. "I guess in strange places when they are under interrogation it's only appropriate. Like dear old English gentlemen out on the marshes being harassed by the king's guard. You know those old classics."

"Have your read this book?" Tom asked, pointing to *The Hung Jury*.

"Yes, I prodded though it."

Tom waited a long moment, afraid to ask, contemplating whether to ask at all.

"What did you think?"

"Well, the best I can say about it is, it's not over there, not yet anyway." He pointed to his fireplace. Ashes were lying in heaps smothered by books with pages opened and turned face down. They had been set afire but had failed to burn completely.

"The story was plausible. I wish someone with the slightest talent had written it." He studied Tom's face again.

"It was totally amateurish. I was amazed that he had a good theme. He had a beginning, middle, and an end." He exhaled in frustration. "Some people don't know when to stop; they just ramble on until you have to end it yourself." He pointed to the fireplace again.

"He was clumsy in his transitions. I just wanted to reach out and grab him and say just put a period on it, write Chapter 10, or whatever, and start a new topic!"

Tom watched him closely. He was old; he lived in filth and everything around him was in decay, but his words were like steel. They cut him to the bone. It was all true. He was an amateur, nothing more. Wilhelm was laid open here. There was no hiding. No pretense. It was dirty and empty, and he was alone. There was nothing to be arrogant about. His honesty was beyond scrutiny. *The Hung Jury* was as he saw it - a good story written by a novice.

Tom stood, quietly dreading Wilhelm's words. The old man's gaze was no longer uncomfortable for him. He accepted the criticism. He had known it all along but didn't want to face the truth. *The Hung Jury* was a piece of shit.

Then, unexpectedly, Wilhelm asked, "Did you write this book, boy?"

"Yes, I did, how did you come by a copy of it? How did you know?"

"I got my ways. Look around here. There hasn't been a word written in the English language I haven't read." He shuffled over to the computer with the mule's backsides shining on the screen. He swung a magnifying screen around to cover the monitor, then scooted his chair and eased his decrepit body down. He started pushing the keys circling around them as though his fingers might never come down.

"They have this thing they call the internet, you know." He pecked on the keys with his head tilted back to view the monitor through his glasses. "So, you're a high school dropout, among other things," he said as though he might be the interrogator now. "You do know that once you submit your name to print your life is an open book, don't you, boy?"

Tom stood rigidly looking at Wilhelm, feeling somewhat under attack. "It says that about me in there?" he asked.

"That and other stuff. It goes on to say you graduated from a half-assed college in Springfield, Illinois. How'd you do that? GED?"

"Maybe I should go," Tom said.

"You're getting a little long in the tooth to be starting a new career. Aren't you?"

Tom thought he was still young enough to be called boy, but too old to start a writing career. "I'll be going now," he said. His brow was beginning to furrow.

"Don't leave; don't you want to soak up any of my knowledge, boy? I mean, for Christ sakes, there's plenty of room for you to expand!"

Tom had come to that point - that place where he would boil over: that Webster breaking point, the batting Gilbert's head with a Louisville Slugger breaking point. "You're just like they said. You're a mean old son-of-a-bitch. Look at this place, you live like a derelict and everything here is a piece of shit! I'm sorry I came here. You're a bitter old bastard!"

Wilhelm stared at Tom, but he wasn't angry or even shocked or even surprised.

Tom started for the door. Wilhelm shouted in his feeble voice, "Wait! Don't be so sensitive. You're right. I'm a miserable old bastard. I'm glad you pointed that out."

Tom looked at Wilhelm in disbelief.

"Ask me anything, boy. I'll answer."

Tom was astonished but his ire had diminished. Wilhelm shuffled over to him. taking him by his elbow and escorted him back through the maze to the table in the clearing.

"Sit down please, have your tea."

Tom watched him curiously.

"I'm a miserable old son-of-a-bitch, a bitter old bastard, just as you said. I'm everything you said."

Tom was silent. The situation had drastically changed. He was no longer a man looking for information or trying to find answers. It was entirely something else. It was emotional. In the few moments since they had met, they had touch on subjects so intimate that they could hate each other. It was surreal.

"Why are you so destitute? Why are you here – in this place?"

"My condition here is without hope. I'm abandoned here. I'm lost, boy. I'm truly lost."

Wilhelm's voice was quivering, and his skin was grayer than it had been before. As he spoke his features suddenly became twisted and tortured.

"How can you be? I'm no expert, but I'm guessing that five best sellers and several other popular books in the short time you were writing would be millions if not more."

"Money is not my plight. I've got money, more then I need. I've got an apartment in downtown Chicago, I assure you, I am not without means. I haven't been to Chicago since 1969, but I pay the lease every year. My problem is I'm imprisoned here. I'm wretched and laid low here but none of it has to do with money. He covered his face with his hands. "I'm lost, boy, I'm truly lost. I lie in my bed each night praying that I will be dead before morning." He raised his head and ran his hands through his gray straw-like hair. Tears filled his eyes. "I came here to research a story for a book. I thought I'd be here for six months. I bought this little house to stay in while I was here. I didn't know when I wrote the check it was my prison. I didn't know I was losing my soul. I'm cursed and empty."

Tom was confused and weary. He didn't want Wilhelm to open up his heart, but he had to listen.

"You can go to Chicago," he said.

"No, I can't. I can never leave. I own half the cemetery and I intend to use it. I can never go." "Why can't you just leave?" Tom was almost imploring him.

"I came here when I was 39 years old. I had five best sellers in print and nine others in bookstores.

I was at the top of my career. I had just come back from France and I spent a few months in St. Helena, California, Chicago, and then here to this godforsaken place. I was only on an excursion. I was researching a story about a black man who killed a white man with a hammer. It changed my life forever!" Tom wasn't concerned about the story or the research. He was concerned about Wilhelm's self-imposed jail.

"I met a young woman who was working in a card shop downtown."

"Is the card shop still there?"

"No, it's closed now, but that's where I met her. She helped me select a card. She was a simple looking girl, not striking at all but I liked her. The way she talked was unique. She was straightforward about everything. I couldn't stop thinking about her. I went there several times just to see her, buying cards I never sent. She was married to the Associate Judge of Van Buren County. These judges around here don't make a lot of money, but I suspected she worked just to occupy her time. She had three children, all boys. She was 24 years old. My wife was in Chicago. I'm ashamed but I was determined to spend time with her. My wife loved me dearly. If I go to hell it will be because I crushed and devastated her." He stopped and sought out a dirty handkerchief to wipe his eyes. His tears were flowing freely.

"I loved my wife, I truly did, and the fact that I ruined her life is the heaviest burden I've had to carry. I'll carry that disgrace to my grave. God forgive me, I could not stop myself, and even at this moment I would crush her again, and that is atrocious." He placed his handkerchief in his sagging robe pocket.

"I went to the card shop each week finally taking her for walks in the park down past the courthouse. One day I kissed her. She said, 'I love you'. I laughed and said, 'You can't love me. You don't even know me'. I was wrong. She was in love with me. She stayed with me for 22 years. She didn't want a divorce because of those kids so we saw each other discreetly every day. Her husband never asked her in all those years if she were unfaithful. I wondered about that the entire time we were together, and to this day I can't believe it. My only thought is that you could line up 200 women and you would guess 199 times before you would guess her as being the unfaithful one. She was so thoughtful and direct about everything. I'm sure if he had asked her, she would have told him everything."

Wilhelm went on to describe her as a loving and unassuming woman with the kindest eyes. When he spoke of his indiscretion, he couldn't do it without completely blaming himself. Though the guilt hung in the deep lines beneath his eyes, he indicated that her guilt was greater. She was ashamed right from the beginning, but she couldn't stop herself. At first, he only wanted sex and it was good, but he could have walked. He could have ended it. She could not. She was completely enamored with him, but she didn't want to be. The guilt was there, and she wanted to stop loving him right from the beginning, but she clung to him and wouldn't let him go. He withheld his love for years before he broke. She asked time and again why he couldn't love her in the same way and then he finally did – completely.

"I was married, and I fought it but I fell in love with her. I don't believe any man could get as close to her as I did without falling in love with her." He paused, looking at the floor as he ran his hand through his hair. "There was something about her that cannot be explained. She's just a little better than anyone else in this world. She's just on a higher level than the rest of us." He paused again and breathed deeply. "After a while my love was so deep that the thought of being without her was unbearable. I knew there would never be a good end to it so I hoped it would go on forever. And it has for me." His voice was now calm, and his words were mechanical and clear. "She got pregnant and had a baby girl. She never asked for a dime from me, but she knew I would have given her anything. She was careful never to use the judge's money for the baby. She thought that was hypocritical. She totally supported that child with her meager income. How the judge didn't see that I will never know. She loved that child in an uncommon way. When her daughter was 16 years old, she was 45. I loved her more then, than I did when she was 25. That was when she delivered that dreadful unbearable news that she was too overcome with guilt and regret to continue our relationship. It was impossible for her to teach her daughter about sex, chastity and virtue when she herself was involved in an illicit affair. She was as devastated as anyone I have ever seen, but I was devastated more. I loved everything about her. I loved her bushy eyebrows, her smooth skin, her crazy-looking eyes and her funny little nose. I loved the way she walked and talked, the way she smelled, and I loved every thought she had in her head. The fact she wanted to leave me was a thing to be admired, but it was so painful I couldn't appreciate what she was trying to do. I didn't accept it. Several times I followed her and cornered her, and she was never upset with me. She was so kind, and so wonderful. She would just quietly say over and over again, "I love you, but this has to end." She was never harsh, and never strayed from that kindness. She vowed that she loved me and would always love me, but she was sticking to her guns. It was over."

Wilhelm stopped and sobbed as though his desolation had been only moments ago. He was so close to that painful moment that it was palpable. He wiped his eyes and blew his nose, completely engulfed in his misery.

"I drove past her house night and day endlessly watching her home. It was somehow comforting just to see her house, to know she was there. I prayed for a miracle, but none came. The last time I saw her she was watering flowers in her yard. I stopped at the intersection and watched her. She turned to go inside then she saw me. She stood up slowly, looked at me and covered her heart and sighed. She mouthed the words, *I love you*. There was pain and, even worse, pity in her eyes. I completely broke down. I drove to the park and stopped there crying like a baby. I contemplated walking in front of a transfer truck or jumping off a building. I was 60 years old. I was about your age, and my life was over," he said.

Tom watched Wilhelm with a frown. "With all due respect, sir, that sounds more like obsession than love."

"Obsession! Of course, it was an obsession. The obsession Jay Gatsby had for Daisy Buchanan paled by comparison. Of course, it was an obsession. I continued to drive by her house until I couldn't get a driver's license – too decrepit. I would drive by it now if my body would accommodate me. The judge left here five years ago. He's in Naples, Florida. He left her but I'm still here. I can't leave her."

"Why don't you go to her, then?" Tom asked.

"She's out there," Wilhelm pointed a bony finger towards the crystal-clear bay window, a window wiped clean for an unobstructed view. Tom looked out. Molly was situated on her knees pulling weeds from around the newly blooming mums. The sun was setting, and her hair was ablaze with light as the sunbeams danced as though glimmering on a halo. Tom watched her momentarily.

"Your wife is lovely, boy, but that's not what I'm pointing to. It's beyond her."

Tom looked past the blacktop road to the pathway leading to the cemetery,

"She's in the cemetery, boy!"

"She's dead?"

"She was 54. Can you imagine that? A woman so young, so much needed and loved, dead at such a young age?"

His face was twisted in pain and even now his heart was breaking. He placed his arms across the table, placed his face in his arms and wept.

Tom stood silent among the books stacked four feet high. The clutter was bewildering. Standing motionlessly, surveying the alleyways through the rooms and the mold and breathing the odor in the air,

Tom Webster was without a comforting word. It was so dark that a beam of light couldn't find its way in, but these were the least abhorrent of misfortunes within Wilhelm's home. The most tragic and loathsome entity in the house was Wilhelm's soul. That part of him that had died had left a hole so wide it had become an abyss. The old man wept, and moaned forgetting Tom was there, then finally he spoke her name.

"Susan, Susan, Susan, I can't do this without you. I can't, I can't. Susan I will never have peace, please let me die now."

"I should go. I'm sorry," Tom said, placing a hand on Wilhelm's folded arms. "Son, please don't go. I'll be okay if you'll give me a moment."

Tom waited and Wilhelm wiped his eyes with the skirt from his robe. He pried himself from his chair and rearranged the teacups. He took up his cane and shuffled through the canals to a side room. Soon he shuffled back and seemed to have recovered his composure. He carried a blue binder that appeared to be at least six inches thick. He placed it upon the table as though he were seating a sacred document upon an altar. Tom read the cover. It said, *SUSAN*, by Edwin Wilhelm.

"I'm bringing this to its final destination. I'm sure I won't last much longer to stew in my own misery. I couldn't bear to have any publicist lay an eye upon it. It's going over there." He pointed to the fireplace.

"If you'll please stay with me until it's gone, a pile of ashes if you will."

Tom glanced out the squeaky-clean window. Molly was there with dirt to her elbows. An orange glow shimmered on the tree line and the gravestones in the cemetery casts long shadows.

"I'll stay," he said.

"I'll tell you some things about your story, and maybe a few things you don't want to hear, but hopefully you will indulge me."

Tom had completely forgotten his purpose there. The intensity and depth of the misery and the obsession and the animosity and finally the easing and the relinquishing of the agony had consumed him. For Wilhelm the bitter fruit he had gathered for those 58 years was up in smoke as the sun dipped below the horizon.

As the thick blue binder smoldered in the fireplace, Wilhelm gathered his thoughts then spoke. "There's a little bookstore in Fremont alongside the square. Next to the store there's a barber shop. An old man like me is there every day sitting on a bench out front. He'd be better off to give up the ghost himself. He's barely hanging on. He knows something about your story. I've heard him talking about it. I disregarded it believing it to be a lie like most lies I hear around here."

"How – How can you –?"

"How does a feeble old man like me get that far away from the rat's nest he lives in?" He looked at Tom sympathetically. "I have a man who takes me places. He can't read a lick, but he can drive. I don't know how he got his driver's license in the first place, but he has one. He takes me to this little bookstore, and I leave the very best of my books there. I talk to the woman who owns the store. I think she's very beautiful."

Wilhelm stopped and contemplated his next statement. An indescribable expression was etched on his face.

"Would you look into my eyes and study them?" He asked softly.

Tom looked. His eyes were extraordinarily clear for a man his age. They were blue, like the sky when you're in a plane at 14000 feet, or the blue at the top of a mountain.

"I want you to know this; and so help me God, you are the only living person who I'm allowing the observation." Tom waited, looking into Wilhelm's eyes, becoming uncomfortable, but for a reason unknown to him, he felt obligated.

"Go into that little bookstore. When you see these eyes again you will know the woman wearing them will soon be a billionaire. I don't know why I want you to know this, but I do." Wilhelm scooted his chair sideways to stare at the dwindling fire.

Tom placed his hand on the old man's shoulder as he turned to leave. Just as he opened the door to exit Wilhelm spoke again, softly and considerately. "Son, when I wrote my first book. they all found their way to the dump table at Dollar Henry Stores, and subsequently to the incinerator behind the Dollar Henry Stores, if that's any encouragement to you. I've read books that were worse than yours that are somehow still in print, God only knows how."

"Would that be an endorsement?"

"I wouldn't exactly call it that," he smiled, "Goodbye, son."

"Goodbye, sir." Tom closed the door.

Chapter VII

As they drove back to Van Buren Tom was floundering. He didn't know how to characterize his encounter with Wilhelm. Somehow, he believed he was more than an interloper in Wilhelm's life. He was encumbered with Wilhelm's emotions and grief, and he didn't enter there willingly but had been drafted into it. It was as though he knew him from the beginning. He found himself rambling on, trying to describe Susan to Molly, but his efforts were taking him further away. How could he describe a woman who was so graceful that she enveloped him and engulfed his will with quiet ways and honest demeanor, and with the same goodness crushed him and destroyed his will?

Molly pondered Tom's rambling statements, occasionally watching his face with intense curiosity. Finally, he stopped. He hadn't finished but simply come to a point where he didn't have words to go on.

Finally, Molly spoke, "What kind of woman would take a man's soul, and I mean that as a question not as a criticism, so completely as to consecrate their love, but to eventually extinguish his identity? I would think she might have innocently extracted the best of everyone she touched. They were cemented together in her mind without the physical attachment. It was real without the touching or being in each other's physical contact, but he couldn't reconcile that in his mind. He needed the touch, the smell, the taste to encapsulate his love. In the absence of that he became obsessed. She went on to love him silently and without strings for the sake of others, but still dedicated to him. I think her love was pure. His love was adulterated by a selfish desire."

Tom watched her face as she explained her thoughts. How could she be so smart? Wilhelm would suffer on without Susan, but she didn't suffer. In her mind, love was still alive. On the other hand, he had lost her and he became the walking dead.

Their conversation had brought them back to Van Buren, but it was too late to engage in other pursuits. They drove back to Farmington and acquired a hotel room.

Tuesday morning, they drove to Fremont and located the bookstore with the barber shop next door. It was closed and there was no elderly man sitting on a bench outside. Tom feared the gentleman might have found what Wilhelm had prayed for himself and was kind enough to pray the same for this old gentleman, considering his age.

Fremont was a mirror of Van Buren, small, quiet, frozen in time, and the residents were content with their existence. If it had a courthouse sitting on the square it could have been the same town. There was one exception; there was an elephant buried in a vacant lot in the middle of town, with a brass placard marking the spot. She had been struck by lightning forty-eight years ago during the fall festival and was buried there to avoid the logistics in moving her.

They went into the bookstore and found tables and a coffee maker brewing on a countertop with donuts and rolls available for customers. A brown-haired woman with glasses who might have been in her late 30s was attending a cash register. The shop was empty. A TV set was mounted high against a wall for those who might be taking advantage of the condiments, and it was tuned to CNN. The coffee and donuts were free for the taking.

The woman smiled as they bid her good morning. She offered coffee, advising them to help themselves. The store was quaint, with oil floors, brick walls, large windows and live plants tenant upon every windowsill. The morning light permeated the aisles and dust glowed in the sunbeams. In the alcove offering the coffee, fresh roses were placed generously about and framed black and white photographs hung on the walls. Tom noticed one photograph of a young woman being held closely by a man in a black robe.

As they sipped their coffee Molly studied the plants and roses. The cashier came to them with a warm smile. "We have everything here in alphabetical order under the authors name except for the newly released books, and this is a list of those. They're in the first aisle against the wall," she pointed.

"This is a beautiful store," Molly remarked cheerfully.

"Thank you."

"The flowers and live plants are wonderful. It's a great idea." Molly turned her open hand out and gestured with a fanning motion.

"I'm sorry to say, I won't be here much longer. My lease runs out in December and I'm not sure I can stay."

"Oh, why? It's such a great place!"

"Truthfully—money. People around here don't read as much as they used to."

Molly directed an I-told-you-so smile at Tom.

Suddenly the woman stopped talking and put her hand lightly over her mouth.

"Oh, my God. Mr. Wilhelm died!"

A CNN reporter positioned in front of Wilhelm's dinky dilapidated brick home speaking into a microphone gestured with his hand and directed viewers to look at the ambulance and emergency personnel milling about. The volume was down but the scroll across the screen in broken sentences reported that the eccentric world-famous novelist Edwin Wilhelm had died sometime during the night.

The store owner fetched the volume control and turned up the sound. The reporter went on to describe the house and the grounds with a practiced astonishment and interjected his newfound knowledge of Wilhelm's weird behavior. Another reporter interviewed the rural mail carrier who had found his body. A different newscaster from the studio reported on Wilhelm's billions, going into great detail about his best sellers and then expanded on his investments in Microsoft in the 80s and other technology-related industries during the 60s and 70s.

They interviewed psychologists and sociologists relating to psychotic behavior and they analyzed Wilhelm's mental state, and ended totally astounded by his condition, comparing him to other reclusive billionaires like Howard Hughes.

The bookstore owner, whose name they learned was Joy, watched the screen with interest.

She bit her fingernail and sadness was born upon her face. Still with her back to them, she said, "He came in here now and then. He donated the books he had read. He was very nice."

She turned and removed her glasses. When her eyes met Tom's, he recalled his weird exchange with Wilhelm about his mountain-sky-blue eyes. For an instant Tom froze. He was looking into Wilhelm's eyes. He turned to review the pictures on the wall. The woman with the judge was Joy. He undoubtedly was her father, or at least to say he was Susan's husband.

They were all quiet. Neither Tom nor Molly mentioned Tom's encounter with Wilhelm. They finished their coffee and went back onto the street.

"You didn't even leave her a tip, and she's having money problems," Molly said.

Tom didn't go into his reasoning, but he didn't think money was her problem. She would have to contend with a different dilemma now.

After questioning a few people lingering on the street they found the barber shop was closed for a funeral, and to their good luck, if any can be found whenever someone is going into the ground, it was not the old man they sought.

Tom questioned a few people about the dead man incident and was hitting a dead end. He recalled Wilhelm's characterization. He was going around like a bumbling idiot asking people he didn't know stupid questions.

Molly visited the various antique shops, but she clearly wasn't happy. She didn't complain but frequent sighs and rolling of her eyes in their sockets left no guessing. Tom was not exasperated but he was impatient. This was time wasted and it might be better spent if he just called it a day. He suggested driving to Ste. Genevieve County to visit the wineries.

Their promenade across the countryside was an odyssey. Tom was born ten miles from Crown Valley Winery in a rundown shack that was long ago torn down. He reminisced as they went, pointing out the changes, declaring that house to be different, and this other house the same, and another house gone completely. They had been to the wineries in California and Tom compared the scenery here in Missouri with a romantic inclination, stating that it was more beautiful here than in Napa Valley. He thought Crown Valley and Chaumette were equals to most wineries in California, too. He and Molly had been to Napa Valley and toured the west coast.

Any conversation about California usually led to Satuii Winery. It was their favorite California vineyard. The Mediterranean buildings and the tasting house; the gardens and outbuildings; the sunset and the golden glow had all settled upon them in the most amiable way, leaving them totally enchanted.

Molly had wandered into the vineyard and walked between the vines, pulling large plump grapes and sampling them at her leisure. Tom was nervously anticipating her eventual apprehension when an older man approached her. He was wearing a blue work shirt and jeans, carrying two buckets.

Light brown hair eluded his cap and fluttered in the breeze. He placed his buckets on the ground and went to Molly. Her eyes expressed surprise and impish connivance. She covered her mouth as she chewed the illicit fruit, examining the man as he approached. Relief was revealed in her smile as he extended an offer for her to eat all the grapes she wanted. He gave her a short tour, describing the grapes, explaining how these grapes would make wine by themselves and others were to be mixed to create a different vintage. It was very technical, and he was remarkably professional in his presentation. When he was gone, they both commented how lucky the winery was to have such a devoted and congenial employee. When they went into the tasting room, they were surprised to see Darrell Satuii's picture hanging prominently in the great room. He and the work shirt, blue jeans clad hired hand, were one in the same.

Tom thought about the incident, remembering Molly, beautiful in the golden glow of the afternoon sun, in the autumn haze, listening intently as Satuii educated her in the art of making wine. She was as comfortable and at ease there as a cat in a window soaking up the sun on a blustery day. Satuii or anyone would have been lucky to have found someone in that grain. She, on the other hand, had been paired with a man who was born in a house with dirt floors and no running water. What a contrast.

A Long Road to Redemption

When they arrived at Crown Valley it was midday. They were surprised by the activity. It was a weekday and it was usually quiet. But today a three-piece band was playing on the veranda. Wine glasses were clinking and raised voices created a low drone. They weren't unhappy to see more vibrant activity; Tom liked a lively party, and Molly enjoyed the music. The winery is situated in a most beautiful place with rolling hills and pastures, sloping hillsides adorned with grapevines with buffalo grazing on the descending slopes below. The music is always soft and never overwhelming. The main building is stone, encircled by a large veranda and an outside complex with fire pits and barrel rooms affixed to the corridors.

Molly went immediately to the gift shop. Tom migrated around to the veranda overlooking the vineyard and the pastures. The band was playing Brown Eyed Girl, imagine that!

He ordered two glasses of Moscato Di Asti, one for himself and the other intended for Molly. He sauntered around studying the people and sipping his wine, then finally sipping Molly's wine. In the corner near the steps to the barrel room he saw an older black gentleman sitting on the stone wall. He was distinguished-looking, wearing an expensive tailored suit, a white shirt and red tie. His face seemed familiar. Tom casually approached the gentleman, pacing about, looking out into the vineyard haphazardly, working his way closer hoping he could strike up a conversation. He finally sat upon the stone wall near the man.

"Nice day, huh," he said.

"Yes, it is," was the answer, but he looked at Tom sideways, not suspiciously but with a certain curiosity.

"You look familiar to me. Do I know you?" Tom asked.

"I don't know, are you from around here?"

"No, not really, I was born here but I've been gone for 45 years now."

"Ste. Genevieve?"

"No, St. Mary's Landing, just seven miles down the road."

"No! I was born in St. Mary's Landing too!"

They looked at each other, both smiling, both examining the others features.

"My name's Tom Webster."

"No! No way, you're not Tommy Webster!"

A broad smile crossed his face. It was a smile that said, "You know me." It was a smile Tom had seen many times.

"Joe! Joe Dalphiet! That can't be you. You sound so different!"

They laughed and hugged each other, then laughed and hugged again. Tom took Joe by his shoulders and pushed him back and studied his face.

"Joe, your face is the same, you're old like me, but your face is the same. But you sound different."

"You know I'm older than you Tommy. I'm Glen's age so I'm supposed to look old, but what's all this gray here on the sides." He brushed a finger along Tom's temple.

"My hair's all white like Moses," he stated, still wearing his enormous grin.

Tom again marveled at how different Joe talked. It wasn't his voice but his words and his accent.

"Tommy, I've been in St. Louis all this time. People there don't care how you sound. Now I love St. Mary's Landing. It's my home - in my mind, you know. But down there they want you to sound all "corn pone." They don't want you to speak any different than any regular nigga. You has to know whae yo place is," he said dropping back into his black accent.

"Mr. Willy's dead, I guess," he said, quickly changing the subject.

Tom agreed.

"Miz. Irene too?"

"Yes, both gone."

"I remember she ran me out of your yard more than once. Me and Glen would be passing words, you know like kids do, and she'd yell, Joe, get your black ass out a here! I'd get too."

Tom smiled.

"She'd call me in for dinner too, more times than I can count. That was uncommon in those days."

A warm feeling came over Tom. He wondered if it was the wine or this chance meeting with an old friend. He thought about the sawmill and how Joe fit into his Great American Novel. He recalled a day in August so long ago. The dust from the log yard was deep and the haze hung thick in the air. The saw in grand fashion was ripping through the cottonwood logs and sap poured out into the sawdust pit below. Boards fell away from the saw in regular intervals, wet and heavy. The mill was set under a vaulted tin roof and the heat, already unbearable, was intensified. A mighty diesel engine powered the pulleys, wheels and belts. The carriage ran to and fro from end to end on rails, clattering and clanking rhythmically as enormous logs gave way in one-inch parcels until gone.

Tom's dad, Willy Webster, was at the helm controlling the levers and power with skill and ease. In this capacity he was an artist at work. In life he had come up short but here in the dust and the heat and the noise he was king. Willy's brother Arthur was there at his side. He was there as he had been for several years. Arthur had been injured in a truck/train accident and had brain damage. Sometimes he seemed to be himself, but usually he was visibly impaired. As they said in those days, he just wasn't right. Willy had watched over him since the day he was injured. When Willy worked, Arthur worked. When Willy was idle Arthur was idle too. And so it was until Arthur died in 1973.

Black youthful bodies, shirtless and sweating, hustled and hurried, sliding boards away from the saw, pushing them along rollers in an endless parade from the saw to the end of the mill where 13-year-old Tom Webster maneuvered them onto flatbed wagons. The wagons were situated four in a row. When a wagon was filled to its capacity Nathaniel Hamilton hitched his mule team (two huge gray bucks) to the wagons and pulled them away. The mules pranced and shuffled into position to exercise leverage then left with a dust cloud mounting behind them. Another wagon was then rushed in to fill the vacancy. The year was 1961.

Nathaniel and his mules were reminiscent of another era. He was in his eighties. He walked stiff legged and feeble. He usually wore a three-day beard and his black face made his white whiskers glitter in the sunlight. He was ill-tempered and seldom spoke to anyone. He had killed a man with a hammer when he was younger, but nobody knew the details. He brought his ravaged body in day after day and he and his mules never faltered. He didn't want to be bothered and the other workers knew not to irritate him.

The sawmill was hard work and not suited for the faint at heart. When a new employee came to work bets were made and money won and lost on how long he might last. What hour would he fall out? Those who stayed an entire day were few, a whole week even less. Those who remained were usually black, uneducated and poor. Willy, Arthur, and Tom were the only whites. Nathaniel was not the only person around who was not to be trifled with. Joe Dalphiet was a strong, energetic, physically fit young militant. He had worked in the mill most of his formative years but found better employment and moved on. Occasionally Joe came back to visit, harass and laugh with his brothers who were still there. Joe worked in St. Louis but somehow found time to come back to hang around. Joe laughed and joked a lot. His two older brothers Sonny and Richard were there, and Frankie, another man they claimed as their brother: a kid who had moved in with them when he was ten years old and never moved out.

There were 17 Dalphiets and they were all crammed into a little shanty they called the slab shack. It was located near the lumber yard. There wasn't a blade of grass or a plant in the yard. There was an old tire swing close by for the younger kids to play on. There were at least ten stray dogs that lounged under the tree and near the house where it was shaded. The house was sided with the bark portion of the tree where it had been cut away from the log and these slabs were irregular in width and thickness. There was no way of fitting them together to get a seal so large gaps were left standing open. There wasn't a location on that house where you couldn't see through from one side to the other. Scrap lumber was plentiful so in the wintertime their wood stove was stoked to the hilt and outside the escaping heat shimmered in the cold air.

There were stackers in the lumber yard who placed the lumber in various locations depending upon the length of the boards. Nathaniel Hamilton hauled the lumber to the yard with his mule team. He left a full wagon and returned the empty to the mill.

One hot August afternoon Joe came to the mill to visit his brothers while they were working. He was mischievous but never disruptive. He was likely to join in, laughing, shouting, and in good humor ridiculing the others, but he also rushed around stacking lumber, carrying slabs and rolling logs onto the carriage. Everybody liked it when Joe came, even Willy. He had said on more than one occasion that Joe was more fun than a barrel of monkeys. Willy was a fearless man, but he never made that same reference when Joe was around. Joe was good-natured, but he was sensitive about even innocent inferences.

After Joe had been there for about a half hour Willy cut the diesel engine, shutting down the mill to sharpen the circular saw. Tom knew it would be about 20 minutes, so he jumped onto a lumber wagon to catch a ride with Nathaniel to the lumber yard. He knew the lumber stackers and liked to catch up on gossip. Joe had left his car at the lumber yard when he arrived, so he took a ride too. Tom was just a kid and Joe treated him like a kid. It didn't make him any difference that Tom was a white boy. In those days whites and blacks didn't socialize. Joe immediately warned him that sitting on wet lumber would give him piles (hemorrhoids.)

"You gonna stay in the mill until you is an old gray wolf like Willy?"

"No, I don't think so, maybe I'll work at the billfold factory," Tom said.

"You know I'z gett'n rich in St. Louie, maybe I get you a job when you grows up."

"I ain't gonna be a city slicker," Tom argued.

"They's hos in St. Louis; but you wouldn't know bout that now, would you?" he laughed.

Tom was embarrassed but he laughed too. He didn't know a thing about girls, much less whores.

The sap in the green lumber soaked through their jeans so they both jumped off the wagon before they reached the lumber yard. Joe's car was blocking the narrow entrance between the stacks preventing Nathaniel from getting the wagon between them. Joe ran towards the car to move it but just then he saw his sister Anna. She had not seen Joe when he arrived because he had gone straight to the mill. Anna was sixteen and fully developed. When she saw Joe she bounced on her toes excitedly. Tom watched Anna's anatomy responding to her excitement. Nathaniel was watching too as Joe ran past his car and went to Anna, but he wasn't garnering the same effects as Tom. A grisly scowl flashed across his features. His hat was usually pulled down to shade his face but now he pushed it back and his black eyes glared at Joe.

"Hey nigger, you need to move yo car," he snapped.

Joe glanced over his shoulder and laughed hysterically. He and Anna continued to talk and hug.

Joe wasn't even offended by Nathaniel's remark.

"Nigger, you better move yo car," Nathaniel bellowed!

Joe continued to ignore Nathaniel and it enraged him even more. Nathaniel paced stiff-legged, shoving his huge black hands into his overall pockets.

In his anger he flapped his hands violently and the ragged denim shook over his buttocks and bony legs. He stomped around in the dust, kicking periodically, cursing and mumbling. At some point in his rage he forgot he was in his 80s, feeble and ravaged. At that time he became the angry young man who had killed a man with a hammer. He started at Joe with his fist doubled, spewing obscenities and spit, and growling indistinguishable noises. He raised his fist, bringing all his energy forward to administer a blow to Joe's face. Joe reached out and caught his bony old hand in mid-air. Joe laughed but this time his laugh had a different sound.

"I got yo nigga now, fool," he said.

Nathaniel struggled to free his hand. Joe squeezed, gritting his teeth, applying all the strength and pressure he possessed, and his anger was unleashed. Nathaniel tried to swing with the other fist, but Joe released his hold and stepped back and fired a right hook to Nathaniel's head. Nathaniel went down like the bag of bones he was. He laid there moaning in the dust.

Joe watched Nathaniel writhing in pain for a moment, then went to move his car and then to the slab shack where the occupants had been watching in astonishment. They didn't celebrate Joe's victory over Nathaniel, but there was a consensus that he had been foolish to go after Joe as he did.

Tom was on the dusty road walking back to the mill, kicking the dust, thinking about the incident.

He supposed he would have to tell Willy what had transpired. He thought Nathaniel might be a little while recovering. Joe ran up behind him laughing about Nathaniel.

"Did you see that ole fool?" he asked.

Tom acknowledged he had, agreeing that Joe had no choice. They walked on together through the log yard and into the mill. Willy was just getting ready to fire up the diesel engine and everyone was taking their places. Joe hurried to Sonny and Richard and related the story to them. They were clearly amused by the account, responding by, slapping their knees and laughing.

Willy eavesdropped periodically glancing at Tom for a reading. Tom just raised his eyebrows, shrugged and hoped he was not asked. During the gleeful narrative Tom saw Willy staring across the log yard with concern in his steel gray eyes. Nathaniel's old green 1949 Chevy pickup truck eased between two log piles and squeaked to a stop. Nathaniel struggled to get out. Once he was on his feet, he stood frail and skinny, but straight and tall with his fist doubled and placed upon his hips. He moved slowly reaching into the truck. Willy looked at Tom.

"Get behind a log," he snapped.

Nathaniel walked stiff-legged towards the mill. His long arms were at his side and in his right hand a .22 rifle rocked back and forth. Joe was alert too, and Sonny, Richard, and everybody in the mill hunted for a hiding place. Arthur was standing between the skids watching, not alarmed or even concerned. Willy remained where he was watching Nathaniel, never taking his eyes off him. Nathaniel raised the rifle to his shoulder and fired. A .22 doesn't have a thundering rapport but to all those present it was plenty loud enough. Some of them shrunk lower in their holes and nudge closer to their logs, but Frankie darted out the back of the mill like a fleeing antelope. Man, he was fast! Willy remained as he had been. Nathaniel came closer, firing three more shots in rapid succession. Joe moved like a cat quickly from one post to another, from a safe place behind a log to a place behind the carriage, and then on to some other vantage point where he would not be shot. He came out and ran past Arthur, a bullet passing between them. Arthur calmly leaned on his cane hook. Joe disappeared behind a lumber stack and was gone from sight. Nathaniel walked into the mill shed, visually scanning the adjacent area. Joe was nowhere to be found. His chin was shoved forward and the hate and anger manifest in his eyes. He glared at the others who were hiding with contempt and his gaze was a challenge to anyone who would dare. He did not look at Willy.

After a few moments it seemed that the danger had passed. Nathaniel dropped the gun to his side and his tension eased. It was then that Joe came back in a dead run. His actions can only be described as cat-like. He was so quick and fast that Nathaniel couldn't react. He hit Nathaniel with his shoulder and knocked him loose from the rifle then pummeled him with a barrage of blows so lightning fast that it was terrifying.

Nathaniel shouted, "Help me," directing his plea to Arthur.

"I didn't help you into that mess," he chuckled. Arthur was standing within arms-length and he smiled as though he were watching a circus act and he didn't move an inch. When it was over, he was in exactly the same place he had been in the beginning.

Joe took the rifle and smashed it against a log, breaking it into pieces, then walked away without saying a word. Nathaniel was lying between the skids bleeding and moaning. Dust and blood mingled to form a paste on his face. Willy walked over to him and asked if he was going to be able to get back to work or should he call Chick Gieler to come with his tractor.

The police were never called, and none ever responded. The sun burned hot and the mill was cranked up to begin making lumber. People were sweating and carrying lumber and slabs and the humidity formed a haze in the air and the sky turned orange behind a cloud. Nathaniel left in his 1949 Chevy truck but soon came back with his mules and started pulling lumber. That was the last time Tom had seen Joe until this moment. It was a grand reunion!

Tom laughed away the time with Joe while Molly shopped for souvenirs. He learned that Joe owned the Uptown Cab Co., and Downtown Limo Service. He had heard Joe's ads on KMOX over the years and he was impressed. It was strange nobody in St. Mary's Landing had ever mentioned that to him. After Joe was gone, he recalled talking to the limo driver in Memphis and remembered the driver had said he worked for his grandfather and they were expanding into Memphis. He checked his wallet for the card and discovered they were one and the same. Small world!

Chapter VIII

On Wednesday morning they were back in Fremont. They found their elderly man situated on his bench with his chin on his chest. It was only 10:00 a.m., but he was already in a gentle slumber. As they contemplated waking him or letting him sleep the barber came out of his shop and eyed them curiously. Tom explained his intentions and the barber advised that the old man was his dad. He came with him every day and stayed until his sister came to pick him up for lunch. He said he knew the story. He had heard it many times over the years; it was a family legend. He knew it by heart, but he thought it would be better told by his father.

He touched the old man lightly. "Daddy, there's some people here to see you."

He was dressed in a brown plaid shirt that hung limply across his shoulders and loose khaki pants. He looked like a little store mannequin that had been pressed into a slumped position and dressed in attire appropriate for a country gentleman, but the clothes were two sizes too big. He blinked a few times then opened his eyes. He turned his hand over revealing his false teeth cupped securely in his palm. He slowly raised them to his mouth and wiggled them in, then bit down to align them.

"I keep 'em in my hand so's not to drop 'em out of my mouth onto the sidewalk," he said quietly, wearing a sheepish smile.

He had a few hairs left but not nearly enough to obscure wrinkles and age spots on his head. He was 85 and wrought by time.

"Did you hear about that feller who wrote all them books over at Van Buren? He died in his sleep."

Tom agreed he had.

"Would you know the name Lawrence Black?"

"Yes, I would. I know it well. I've know'd it all my life," he said feebly.

"Can you tell me the story you know, the one about Lawrence Black?"

He sat staring at the ground for so long Tom thought he might not have understood the question. He started to ask again, and his son shook his head then winked.

"He'll come around," he said.

He cleared his throat and with a soft gentle voice he started, "I can indeed, but my story is more about little Irene Black, more'n it is about Lawrence Black."

Tom was anxious but he didn't want to be rude. He would try to be patient, and polite.

"Sir, first I'd like to know your name. My name is Tom Webster, and this is my wife Molly."

"My name is Wesley Finch. I barbered here for forty years. Everybody knows me around here. My boy, Wes, does the barbering now."

"Wesley, I'd be honored to hear your story."

He studied the sidewalk again then finally started in the same soft and gentle voice. "It was a wet day. We was in school and it rained so as we couldn't go outside for recess. We laughed and played in the schoolhouse till things got out a hand like happens when kids get pent up like that. Teacher made us set real still after that. It quit raining bout half hour before school was out so as we didn't have to walk in the rain. I always walked home with Irene and her sisters, Mabel and Opal, er was it Mabel and Reedy, er, no - Opal. I don't always remember them two, but I always remember Irene cause a what happened." He looked into Tom's eyes and his gaze was soft and considerate.

"We was walking past Richardson's hog lot and this creepy-looking man came across the hog lot and held down the barbedwire fence and stepped over it. He had black whiskers and shabby clothes and he could a used a bath. Irene took notice of him right off and you could see she was afraid of him. Irene was the oldest of them and she took good care of them like she was their momma. I heard her say, oh, no, there's that man again. Irene was two years older than me, so I always listened to her too, you know, like she know'd more."

Tom listened to the story. He knew the way some things were so clear that the smells of those depleted spring afternoons were probably still resonating in the barber's memories like an old photograph. He went on, "We kept a walking and the dirty looking feller follered behind us. After just a little bit he started saying this dirty little song. He said kinda in an evil way, I'm gonna get your ----."

Wesley stopped and looked at Molly and said, "You know what I mean - your you know what."

Molly's mouth fell open.

"We kept a walking and he kept a singing, I'm gonna get your --- you know what. He was getting closer. Irene said, run, and we did, but she kept walking slow like she was before. You know, like she was gonna risk herself for us. Well, I run off down the road, but I hid behind a hog bin in Richardson's hog lot and I watched. That dirty feller come up behind her and he put his arm around her neck. She knocked it off and tried to run but he got her by the arm and pulled her back. He pulled on her and she bit his hand, then he grabbed her dress on the shoulder. She was still trying to get away from him and he tore her dress. He was a holding her, but she kicked him in the leg, and he backed up into the ditch and staggered around out a balance. She was still trying to get away and he was telling her to be still, but she wasn't having it. That's when he draw'd back and hit her right in the face with his fist. She staggered back five feet with the blood streaming, but she was still on her feet. I figured she'd get away then for sure and I kept whispering, run Irene, run, but she didn't. She raised both her fist in the air, and she run at him and hit him about belly high and knocked him clean into the barbed wire fence. He got hung up in the fence and he wallered around a trying to get loose, but that wire had him good. It was a tearing at his britches and his leg was bleeding and he was cussing for all he was worth.

"Irene run out there about 30 feet or so and turned around looking back at him. There was blood on her teeth and her dress was tore but she stood straight up and said, you leave me and my sisters alone! Then she turned and run off."

Wesley stopped and studied the ground again. Tom's eyes were red, and tears were flowing down Molly's cheeks. Wesley's eyes were red too, as though he had never told the story before.

"That's the day little Irene Black became my little hero. When I see all that, I had a feeling come all over me. It was inside me and on my face and in my belly. I didn't know what it was then, but I come to know what it was. It was pride. Being proud to know somebody. I was proud right then and I'm proud now as I'm sitting here. I knew the bravest little girl in this county"

"I can't do anymore of this right now," Molly said, backing up, her face still wet with tears. She walked down the sidewalk pushing a tear aside. Tom followed her putting his arm around her.

"I hope your granddad killed the bastard," she said, laughing and crying at the same time. Tom hugged her and returned to Wesley.

"There ain't a lot more to the story, anyway that I know. I'm not even sure the shooting that took place later had anything to do with that deal. I just know it was the same dirty feller that caught the bullet."

"You didn't see the gunfight then?"

"No, I heard the shots."

"Maybe you could tell me what you heard."

"I didn't go right home after Irene had her deal with that feller. I went on down through Richardson's hog lot and throw'd some rocks at some of them hogs and then down over the hill on that log road that went by Wisdom's sawmill. I splashed in some mud puddles like kids do and just pilfered around for a while, maybe for a half hour or so, then I heard them shots. I heard the first shot and I seen a man running. It was that Scott feller. He run up the hill at the same time the first shot went off. He turned around all excited and he fired off a shot."

"Do you think that was the shot that killed the other man?" Tom asked.

"Like I said before, I don't know who shot him, I only know he was the feller that follered us, but I don't think it was that shot that got him cause that Scott feller was so excited when he was trying to get' er done that he shot at an angle up in the air. There wasn't any human being on the ground in danger a getting shot."

"I'm sorry I got ahead of myself," Tom said.

"Don't be. I'm getting the drift that this is a might more personal to you than for most people judging from the tears and all." He paused and looked at Molly. "Anyways there was them two shots then in just a wink there was a third shot. It was louder, a lot louder, and then it was quiet and I didn't hear no more shooting."

"Did anybody ever question you about it?"

"No, not the Sheriff, nor the Coroner, nor anybody else. My pappy told me to keep my mouth shut about it and that's what I did. I never told it until I was way up and married. I told it in my barber shop many a times since then though."

That was it. There was nothing more. Molly and Tom drove home quietly without talking about Wesley's story. It seemed inappropriate now. It was like being hot and sweaty on a summer day waiting and hoping for a breeze, but when it came it was a cold wind that chilled. They were frigid to the bone.

Chapter IX

This is the story of that fateful day that brought Tom Webster to this moment. On April 28th, 1933 at about 3:15 p.m., Irene Black and her two sisters, Mabel and Opal, along with Wesley Finch, were walking home from school. An unsavory character by the name of Jess Wade was drunk. He was sitting on an abandoned model T Ford in Richardson's hog lot. The weeds had grown up around the junk car, the doors were gone, and hogs had loitered throughout the vehicle leaving dirt, mud and pig shit on the rotting seats and interior. Wade had rested there after having been caught in a downpour. He had been falling-down drunk due to having started drinking in the early morning with his brother-in-law Scott Redding. The two had fought two times and argued fitfully throughout the day. He had run his truck into a ditch a few miles away and had been walking to Wisdom's sawmill to catch a ride home. He had taken refuge in the junk car when he was caught in the rain. He sobered up a bit, but he was still under the influence. He brought his rifle with him from the truck and stashed it in the car. He had been on this road before and knew the little Black sisters walked home past Richardson's. He didn't think about what he might do if they came by, but he recognized the urges building inside. He didn't like thinking about it, and he didn't try to analyze his behavior. He accepted that he was who he was, and he could do nothing about it. He didn't have a plan, but he became excited about the prospect of the girls coming past his location. His imagination took him into the weeds with the oldest girl but any one of them would do. He wasn't looking for romance.

When he saw the girls coming down the road his heart raced, and he could feel the adrenalin surging through his veins. He hurried through the hog lot, grabbed the barbed wire and stepped over into the ditch and then to the roadway. The girls were ahead of him. He loved little girls. He had molested several children in his 28 years and none of them had ever told on him. Most were relatives but that didn't bother him either. He could fondle children and sexually abuse them while their parents were in the same house. He would interact with them later while other adults were present without guilt or remorse. He had reached a point where he wasn't even afraid he would be found out. He thought most kids simply accepted what happened to them and then went on with their lives. He didn't believe his conduct harmed them. He usually threatened to kill them or their parents if they told on him. He told them that he would tell everyone they wanted to be touched and wanted to touch him. He found that to be a very effective way of keeping a kid quiet. It was easy to make them ashamed.

He followed along waiting for the best opportunity singing a little tune he had made up. "I'm gonna get your pussy, I'm gonna get your pussy."

The small girls ran and a little boy too, but the oldest girl stayed behind. He closed in on her quickly. He hoped he could just drag her into the weeds and get it done in a hurry. He grabbed her arm, but she turned and bit him.

"Come on honey, I won't hurt you."

He grabbed her dress, but she jerked away, tearing off her shoulder pad. He clutched her arm and ordered her to settle down and she kicked him. He grabbed her other arm and she kicked him again. He was frustrated and angry. He gritted his teeth and punched her face with his fist. His knuckles were cut, and the blood gushed from her mouth and splattered onto his shirt. She staggered backwards releasing a pained but short gasp, a whimper. He looked into her eyes. She wasn't afraid. She glared at him with anger and determination. She raised both fists and ran at him hitting him hard in the gut. He lost his balance and fell into the barbed wire fence. He was stuck for several minutes. When he was loose, she was gone. He had lost his appetite for sex by then, so he went back to the junk car to retrieve his rifle and headed for Wisdom's sawmill.

At 4:30 p.m., Lawrence Black was unloading logs from his two-ton Ford truck at Wisdom's mill. It had rained several times during the day and one load was all he could manage. The woods were saturated, and he was lucky to get through it the first time.

Lawrence was a big man. He was 6 feet 2 inches tall and weighed about 210 pounds. He was muscle and bone. His strength was legendary in those parts. He was known to have won a bet when he lay on his back in the sawmill log yard while five men tried to hold him down. When the bets were levied and everything was set, he rolled over onto his stomach, then to his knees and with all five men hanging like beggars-lice on a wool coat, he stood up and laughed. He had been involved in one fight and those who saw it would never forget. He had been in a tavern having a beer with a friend when a local bully tried to pick a fight with him. He tried to leave but he was stopped at the door by another man who was with the troublemaker. The witnesses who came forward later said Lawrence was humiliated to tears before he finally broke, but when he did hell's fury was unleashed. He hammered and beat on the two men until his friends feared he was going to kill them. The entire crowd tried to pry Lawrence loose from the man who started the fight, who was unconscious by then. He dragged the defeated man by his hair for a full block while the other patrons hung to him urging him to let him go. He left him lying lifeless in the street. He was never known to fight again, but he never had to, for his reputation and his good nature preceded him.

Today he was frustrated. The ground was too wet to get logs from the woods and that one lone meager load was all he could do. Now his truck wouldn't start. He had spouted "Dag-nab-it," which was his harshest profanity, then he started walking home.

Irene was running like the wind. Blood was oozing into her mouth and was splattered on her dress. She saw her sisters, Mabel and Opal, waiting in the yard. They were wide-eyed and fearful, but relieved when they saw her. Her dad's truck wasn't parked in front, so she thought he wasn't there. She ran past Mabel and Opal and went straight inside. The windows and doors had been closed because of the rain and it seemed muggy. She hurried to the wash basin in the kitchen. The blood was on her clothes and in her mouth, but her nose and lips had stopped bleeding. She wasn't ashamed or afraid, but she wanted to be clean. The dirt wasn't visible, but she could feel it. She couldn't smell the stink, but she knew it was there, it was all over her. It was urgent for her to wash it away. She dipped the washcloth into the water and squeezed out the excess. She started to wipe her face, but before she could a small hand seized her wrist!

"What in tarnation have you done now, Irene?" Addy Black shouted.

Irene pulled away, turning her face towards the wall. Addy gripped her hair and jerked her head backwards to view her face.

"Girl, you're going to be the death of me," she growled.

Irene turned and glared at her mother. Her eyes were fixed and her teeth clenched. There was no fear, no bending, no surrender, just raw determination. Addy's fist held tight as she examined the injuries. At that moment just as Addy's fist had captured Irene's wrist, a huge hand came upon her own. The hand was like steel, but it wasn't. It was callous wrapped upon bone. Addy was barely five feet tall and when she looked up her husband was hulking over her.

"Lawrence, this girl's been up to no good!"

"Let her go, Addy," he said, so low and calm that all agitation and anger was dispatched. Addy dropped her hands to her side and watched as Lawrence gently turned Irene around to face him. He dipped the washcloth into the basin and wrung it out. With Irene's tiny hand enclosed in his he led her into the living room and sat her upon his knee. He wiped away the blood as tears fell hot and profusely.

"I'm sorry, Poppy," she said.

"Irene, you don't have anything to be sorry for. Now run in there and get on some fresh clothes. You don't have to talk about this again."

Irene went to her bedroom and Lawrence went to get his 30 caliber Winchester rifle from the gun rack. He walked to the door, turned and looked back to see his wife with her back to him looking vacantly out the window. Lawrence walked past Mabel and Opal. They watched him, never dropping their gaze.

"Girls, get in the yard and stay there," he stated sternly as he walked up the narrow gravel road and disappeared over the hill.

Irene hurried into the bedroom and found a pair of Lester's jeans. She cinched the belt and tucked away the excess denim and fastened it with a safety pin. She had always wanted to wear jeans like her brothers, but Addy wouldn't allow it. Today she was wearing jeans!

A thunderstorm was looming on the horizon. The storms had been advancing across the sky all day. It had rained in torrents, then it would calm for a while, only later to darken and then the rumbling would begin in the distance to be followed by another downpour. Irene was wrung out by her encounter and she sat wearily watching the horizon. She felt exhausted behind her eyes.

At 5:45 Irene and her two sisters heard a sound like thunder but sharper and clearer. They waited silently and then a softer rumbling peeled off over the horizon, then it was quiet again. A silhouette appeared on the hilltop and a man trotted towards them. His right hand was cupped against his side. Mabel and Opal were sitting on their knees and Irene was dangling her legs from the porch as the man came closer. He started slowing down, becoming unsteady. He came still closer and Irene stood up watching like a little eagle, a guardian over the other two. The man wavered then staggered and stumbled into their yard. Irene clenched her fist and took two steps towards him. Blood dripped across his hand and poured onto the ground. He fell at her feet and rolled onto his back. A bloody hand reached out for her. She stepped back. Pleading eyes met Irene's eyes.

"Help me," he gasped as blood oozed from his mouth. Irene stepped forward watching his face and seeing his chest heaving. "Don't die," she whispered.

A guttural rasping sound issued from his throat. He opened his eyes wide and he was dead. Whatever went through Irene's mind at that moment was never known.

Chapter X

Molly had left her car at Joe's home in St. Mary's Landing the weekend before their dead man adventure. That was where they parted. Molly headed back to Hernando and Tom left for Willoughby Hills. Molly cried again as she did every time they went their separate ways. She could have turned her car north and went home but she was determined to make these changes in their lives. She thought the college needed her and the success of the school was crucial to their future. They laughed about being nickel millionaires trying to beat their checks to the bank, but it wasn't a laughing matter. The truth was that you could be a millionaire on paper and still be broke. They were living proof. She knew little Adi needed her, so she was southbound. Tom always met her halfway when she made the trip home each week or they met at the cabin in Missouri. When she started south, and he went north he would say they were moving away from each other at 160 miles per hour. She didn't like the analogy, but she was sure of him and he was sure of her. Miles didn't make a difference when you are alloyed in steel as they were.

Tom went to the cemetery in St. Mary's Landing. Willy and Irene were buried in the same grave. Everett and Wanda were killed in a car accident in 1967, and they were buried there too. Irene was with them in that crash and so seriously injured that she was given poor odds to live. She survived but lost her right leg. She was fitted with a prosthetic leg that was never comfortable for her, but she learned to walk and became vital in her remaining years. Willy died in 1987 and Irene died in 1993. At Irene's funeral there wasn't enough room in the church for all who wanted to pay their respects. The church was full, the parking lot full and cars were lined up on the roadway. She was loved by everybody she knew. That was an achievement since she didn't avoid unpleasant discussions and she never gave up and she never backed down. Leaving the world with no enemies with that as her concourse was a testament to her character.

She raised ten kids on pauper's wages. She knew how to go into a field and find edible roots and wild plants, and she prepared them and fed them to her children in order to survive. She lived in homes with dirt floors having windows without glass and without running water or electricity. She read to her kids by lamplight and candlelight and washed clothes on a washboard in order to send them to school clean. Aside from her Social Security check she never took a dime from the government. In the end she owned a comfortable home and had money in the bank. She had children who had college degrees and successful businesses, and grandchildren who were pharmacists, investors and teachers. In the weeks before she died her children hovered over her with warmth and affection. Even now from her grave she influenced all their lives.

Tom quit school and left home a month before he turned 16. Life was never unbearable for him being on his own at such a young age. He knew the pang of hunger and the discomfort of not having a bed to sleep in and he could write a book on being broke, but there was never a time or a moment when he doubted he could walk into Irene's home and be wrapped in a blanket of love. He built his life on a lie, a small lie by Molly's assessment, but a lie just the same. Irene never knew Tom lied about his past in any manner. She expected him to stand up and be who he was, admit his mistakes and then make lemonade. That was her way.

What kind of mother would let her 15-year-old son quit school and leave home? Tom would answer—a saint; a woman who would fight for her kids and defend them to her death but would ask them to be upright and self-sufficient. She would want them to be brave and strong and honest. She wouldn't want a son to make mistakes and then lie about it to make life easier.

Tom couldn't turn back the clock. He couldn't take back the punch he laid on the principal's jaw or erase the words he had written on his police application. He wasn't going to give up his interest in Mississippi Tech. He simply wanted to do something to show the world what kind of mother he had. Her life was mundane, her work was tedious and boring, and her worldly possessions were ordinary, but the dead man incident was a tempest. No murder or killing, or the taking of another person's life should be sensationalized, but the dead man incident was sensational. Tom thought that within the story he might find a way to define the character Irene possessed, and write about it. The story was suspenseful and although it was insidious, it was arousing. It was furious and maddening with heroics and villainous behavior. It was set away from the mundane and in the end, it might show just who she was. If he wrote it well, he hoped he might find justification for his own miscues.

He told this all to his mother there in the cemetery standing among the Websters with their granite headstones to mark their graves. He was sure Everett and Wanda would not recognize him and he told them so, but his mother would know him through all his changes, his gray hair, his wrinkles, his false pride and his folly. He wasn't at all afraid that Willy would get up and glaze-over, huffing and puffing with fire flying from his eyes. He loved that old man too. As the sun faded into dusk and the gravestones into shadows, Tom left the cemetery for Willoughby Hills at 160 miles per hour away from his better half; his half of Tom and Molly.

In Willoughby Hills Tom sat in his little office with the curtain free windows looking at the laptop computer Molly had bought him. The sun was shining, and he retrieved a baseball cap to shade his eyes from the glare. Maybe he should consider some curtains, he thought. He opened the lid on the computer and studied it for a long time. He thought about *The Hung Jury*. That story was easy to write. He had lived it. The Great American Novel might be a hair different. The word program was loaded. He circled the keys a few times then started.

"Jenny, of all those I ever loved, I loved you most."

A small framed woman looked over her reading glasses and said, "My name is not Jenny, it's Theresa." He stopped and looked out into the backyard. The old hot tub had been idle for a few years now. A trellis and a fire pit might look good there. He looked back at the computer, hit the delete button then closed the lid. He pushed his chair away from the desk and went for his hammer.

Chapter XI

This is where we find ourselves looking back into the past. It was a morning like many mornings when you want to do something or anything, but doing nothing is easier. The wind off Lake Michigan was keeping the air cool and the traffic on Dearborn Street was light but just the sound of a horn or an accelerator or the squeak of a brake was irritating.

Edwin Wilhelm was pacing around the apartment, first playing a few tunes on the piano, then tuning the radio to an early morning live radio program, then trying to read the Tribune; finally he stopped all efforts in a huff.

He wasn't sleeping well, and he had lost all desire to meet new people. His wife Joanne was in Los Angeles with the kids and he was missing the distractions they provided but glad on the other hand that he didn't have to deal with conversations. He was the most famous writer in America, and he couldn't go to a restaurant or bar without being recognized. At first that was what he wanted, but now his skin had grown thin and all he wanted was to sleep through the night without waking before daylight with a bug in his brain crawling all over his peace of mind. Sometimes he thought he was losing his sanity, but he knew as long as he worried about it, he was still in touch.

Several times this last week he reread an article he had found in a file left in an antique chest of drawers Joanne had drug home from an auction. Edwin Wilhelm was rich beyond his wildest dreams. He had five best sellers in print and money was falling from the sky. He was a small-town boy from Ohio, and he was on a roll. Joanne could have afforded anything on earth she wanted but antiques were her latest fad.

The article nagging at him was from the 1930s. A young black mule skinner had killed a white man with a hammer after the man shot one of his mules. Wilhelm believed racial conditions were at a boiling point. He thought writing a book about racial tensions would be interesting and ahead of an historical upheaval. It was a good story. The young black was set free after a lengthy trial. There were ramifications which made it more interesting. Edwin thought it would make a good book.

The year was 1950. Edwin was 39 years old. He had made his fortune on books and short articles, but wealth had been the byproduct of his efforts. He had always been different. He was a good-looking man - athletic and strong. He was well-liked and intelligent. His problem was that when he was alone his mind would not rest.

He had been arrested several times in his youth for curfew violations, merely by wandering around alone in the dark on the streets just hoping for peace of mind. Finally, he learned he could put his frustrations to bed by writing about them. In the end it made him rich and famous.

Edwin had a brand-new ostentatious Cadillac. It was black and shone like a new dime. It had huge whitewall tires and an AM radio with a search button and a sensor for automatically dimming the headlights. He packed a small bag and a few suits and sports coats and ties. He called the garage and had the car delivered, and in a few minutes, he was headed south en route to Van Buren, Missouri. Five hours later he was stuck in traffic in St. Louis at Cedar & Locust. He made a left turn towards the river and hit Broadway St., then went south. He stopped at Soulard's market. He ate two plums and a banana while he listened to the banjo player who played then waited for donations to be dropped into his hat. People were drinking beer and eating bratwurst. He thought it was absurd to eat sausage sandwiches and drink alcohol for breakfast, but the smells were so inviting that he thought he might write a book with that location as his centerpiece.

He left Soulard's and fought his way through traffic past the Budweiser brewery to Lindberg boulevard to U.S. 61 then south. At 2:30 p.m. he was in St. Mary's Landing, Missouri. The town had only 600 residents, but Wilhelm was impressed with the activity. Every shop was full of people lined up in doorways and waiting on the street to spend their money. He went through town in short order and found a place alongside the road to revisit his map. There was a sawmill puffing smoke and clamoring with activity. The ground was covered with dust and loose bark and logs were lying about haphazardly. The saw was cutting through logs spitting out boards while youthful sweating black men hurrying and hustling to put them on their way before another board fell onto its place. He saw a young woman with two small boys walk past him eying him curiously. She stopped just short of entering the mill, then started preparing something from a brown grocery bag. The thunderous diesel engine halted and Wilhelm watched as several men dispersed. One young man passed near him proceeding to a galvanized can with water and ice.

"Why has the mill stopped?" He asked.

"Mr. Willy's filing the saw."

Wilhelm ventured nearer to the mill. The young woman was sitting on an 8x8 timber among the bark and sawdust. Her feet were bare, and she was wearing dungarees.

The bag she carried was brimming with green leafy plants and she had a small galvanized bucket in her hand.

"Good morning, Miss."

"Miz, I'm married to him," she said as she pointed to a rail thin man who was dragging a file across a huge circle saw. Another man walked towards them carrying a black lunch pail.

"Good morning," Wilhelm said cheerfully.

"It's after lunch," he responded. He looked at the ground, avoiding Wilhelm's

friendly greeting.

Wilhelm looked at the woman inquisitively.

"He's kinda quiet." She said.

Wilhelm studied her face. She was thin with deep black hair and eyes. She had interesting features and it was easy to see she did not suffer a lack of confidence.

"I've never seen a woman wearing blue jeans before," he said smiling.

"I like britches" she said, dismissing the remark.

"My name is Edwin Wilhelm," he said reaching a hand towards her.

She took it. "I thought you was Dwight D. Eisenhower when you came up in that big black car," she laughed.

He thought it was a good thing that she didn't recognize him, but just for a fleeting instant he missed that. How could that happen? For the last three years that was all he wanted, just to be somewhere where nobody knew him. Now for that split second, he thought, hey wait a minute, I'm Edwin Wilhelm. Strange??

She started emptying the bag onto the ground, placing each item systematically in front of her.

"What is that?" he asked.

She appraised the arrangement momentarily, deciding just where to start.

"They're all wild plants. This one here is collard greens, and these are wild onions and wild garlic. These little peach-like things here are persimmons. These are chestnuts."

"They look like buckeyes."

"Well, I know them as chestnuts."

He shrugged. He was from Ohio and he thought they were buckeyes, but he wouldn't argue the point.

"They taste like potatoes when they're roasted"

"Okay."

"This is a horseradish—you have to be all Mexican to hold one of these in your mouth. They're hot. This over here is bacon grease. The little cup has bits I strained from the grease."

"What are you doing with all that?"

"Well, I'm going over there and build a fire," she pointed, "and I'll put these greens in the big bowl, and I'll heat the grease in that big black pan. I'll cut the onions and garlic and dice the persimmons and fry them in the grease. The chopped persimmons will give it just a little sweetness. I'll grate some of the horseradish into the grease for some spice, add pepper and basil. I'll wilt the greens with the grease and sprinkle the bacon pieces on top, then me and him" (she pointed at her husband) "and my boys will eat it."

"It sounds good. How do you know all this? I mean about which plants are edible?"

"I just know," she said.

Nathaniel Hamilton trotted his mule team past them stirring the dust—an aged black man and two beefy mules.

"I was on my way over to Van Buren. I've got a newspaper article about a man who was tried for murder for killing his foreman. He was a mule skinner and he worked in a sawmill. I was wandering if you might have heard a story like that? It happened a long time ago. I found the article in an old chest we bought."

"You can't sling a cat around here without hitting a sawmill," Arthur, the quiet man who passed Wilhelm earlier, piped in. Arthur eyed Wilhelm's expensive watch and his Italian leather shoes and noted his pleated pants with a seam so rigid it was sharp enough to cut.

"Why would you be look'n for somebody who knows all that?" Art asked suspiciously.

Wilhelm was confident that no one would be pestering him for an autograph or asking him to read a manuscript they had written, so he took his case straightforwardly.

"I'm a writer. I write books," he said

"What kind of writer?" The woman asked.

"I write books, you know, novels."

"You said your name was Wilhelm?"

"Yes, Edwin Wilhelm."

"Sorry, never heard the name."

It was becoming frustrating now. Naturally he wanted to be left alone, but he was starting to realize it had been awhile since he was completely unknown, and he didn't like that either. "I'm doing research for a book. I like to know the people and the background of those I write about. I want to write about racial inequalities and prejudice."

The young woman looked at Wilhelm curiously. Arthur looked, too.

"If you're not just a little bit prejudice then you're not paying attention," she said.

Wilhelm looked surprised. This wasn't exactly the south.

"That seems strange coming from you - you don't seem to be a hateful person."

"I'm not going to argue with you about racial things. I should have kept my feelings to myself. I'll just say they're my feelings and I'm not about to change them."

"This story I'm researching – will I run into problems with people over it?"

"I wouldn't think so as long as you don't start preaching."

The two little boys the woman had with her were wrestling and kicking sawdust around. She intervened, putting an end to the topic. When she returned Wilhelm was talking about himself again.

"I've written several books, surely you've heard of *The Raven in The Willow*?"

"I'm sorry. I've never heard of it."

The thin gaunt-looking man filing the saw stood up and dusted the sawdust from his pants. He was finished with the chore and he eyeballed Wilhelm. His gray eyes were piercing and mean-looking. Wilhelm was instantly nervous.

"I'd tell you not to worry about him, but that just wouldn't be right. You should worry about him. His reputation is that he's a dangerous man, and that's putting it mildly."

Wilhelm pondered her remarks. Now wouldn't it be incredible if the country's most famous writer got thumped by a mill hand for talking to his wife. He was wishing for just a little bit of that notoriety he had shunned.

"Maybe I should be looking for Van Buren," he said.

The young woman separated her kids again, then provided directions to the blacktop road that would get him going in the right direction.

Before leaving Wilhelm said, "You can find my books at Dollar Henry. I always give them the first 100,000 copies." He was now determined that they should know how famous he was. He emphasized the number with a raised eyebrow.

"I always give them the first 100,000 because they took a beating on my first book. It's in my contract with the publisher. They always get the first 100,000."

"We don't have any Dollar Henry's around here. That's like a dime store, isn't it?"

"Well, it's a little more substantial than a dime store."

"Well we don't have one."

"Okay, bye." He said.

"Okay, bye." She said.

As Wilhelm drove away the woman emptied her grocery bag onto the ground. Among the greens, the wild onions, garlic, the horseradish that burned like a bee sting, and the persimmons, was a paperback novel. A picture of Wilhelm was on the back. It was *The Raven in The Willow*.

"Is that him that wrote that book?" Arthur asked.

"Yep, that's him alright."

"How come you didn't ask that old boy to write his name on the cover like they do?"

"I didn't want him to get all puffed up." She tore off a piece of the grocery bag and fetched a stubby pencil from her pocket and handed it to her three-year-old. "Stop fighting, Tommy, and take this and go write with it. Write a story about mommy. Maybe you'll be a famous writer someday like Edwin Wilhelm."

As Wilhelm drove down the curving road, he enjoyed the bright sunshine with the wind blowing through the windows. The Cadillac had an air conditioner, but Wilhelm liked the outside air. He didn't think a car air conditioner would ever catch on. People liked to drive with their arm hanging out the window.

Just before he reached the turnoff, he saw a bright yellow sign and several cars in a parking lot. There in full view as big as Mississippi was the Dollar Henry store. He smiled. This was going to be a long trip. As it turned out it was the longest trip of his life.

Chapter XII

The calamity had to start sometime, and it had a beginning. On April 28th, 1933, the morning broke with thunder rumbling and blustery wind stirring the trees and chilling the bone. It was a morning when dawn came creeping over the hills and slowly ascended unnoticed into day. In south central Missouri in 1933 there were hog farms and cattle farms, but loggers and sawmill workers were more plentiful. They filled the woods and mills wearing their unkempt hair and overalls and flannel shirts and brogan shoes. Some wore beards and mustaches, but they all wore their skin like iron. They were calloused and rough and were accustomed to hard times.

Money was hard to come by, but when it rained the beer joints and hog sheds were full and the beer, whiskey and homebrew flowed like water. In the cities, men played stickball and basketball and hovered around burn barrels and talked about football and Friday night fights, but here in these hill towns the men were the Friday night fights. When they were rained out, they were all in for a good time, or bad, however it came down.

Fremont was their town, and it sat near the Black River between two mountains that were covered with red cliffs, looming over a leg of the river. The bluffs were jagged slabs of red tap rock laden with iron ore, pointing skyward, with cedar trees perched on flat landings between the mountaintop and the base below. Ivy and wild vines hung over the protruding edges, cascading towards the river. Cedars grew out of every crack and crevasse, and everything seemed natural to the untrained eye, but the cliffs were manmade, having been carved away in parcels and transported to rock crushers where the iron ore was extracted and hauled away to iron mills. Mother Nature had rounded out the sharp cuts and angles, and now the mountains looked like a small version of the Rockies.

There were homes sporadically positioned on hillsides and valleys and beside one-lane gravel roads leading to the town. They became less scattered until they merged into a small village, but there was never an actual city limit. The residents here were all citizens of Fremont regardless of whether they lived in town, or three miles away. It was a community where everybody knew everybody else. They were all poor, most of them were hardworking well-meaning people, but there were exceptions. Forgiving was easy in Fremont, and sometimes just ignoring bad behavior negated the necessity of going through the process.

Jess Wade and Scott Redding stopped at Wisdom's sawmill where Redding left his truck. They went on together to meet George Darrow. They had been hired by the government to clear trees and brush along Current River. Darrow was under contract and Wade, Redding and two other men worked for him. The sand and gravel along the river would usually support traffic but if it rained the river bottoms would be soggy. Both Wade and Redding had grabbed their rifles so that if they were rained out they would be able to hunt squirrels.

Redding was a small wiry man and he had just turned 23. He was clean-shaven and had fair complexion with blond hair. He was not a wooly, rugged timber jack type, but he had been around the trade all his life. Wade was 28. He was burly-looking with black hair that covered his ears and he wore a three-day beard. His jaw was rounded with a chaw of tobacco at all times. Wade was five years older than Redding, but they spent a lot of time together because Wade was married to Redding's oldest sister Margaret.

Redding knew Wade was ill tempered and mean. He didn't know Wade was sexually perverted and totally without a conscious. Wade had been good to him and he liked him. He had never been unfair or obnoxious to him, but he had seen him agitated and belligerent with others. Today Redding would find out the worm had turned.

They left the log yard taking the gravel road past Lawrence Black's residence. They saw Irene Black and her two sisters and Wesley Finch headed off to school.

"There's them little Black girls," Redding said.

Wade stared at them as he drove by.

"And there's that little Wesley Finch, ain't he some kind of relation to you, Wade?"

"That little fuck'n Wesley Finch," Wade snorted.

They both laughed. Wade because he had a twisted sense of humor about something he had done. Redding laughed because Wade did.

Wesley Finch and his mother had stayed with Wade for a short time. Wesley's mother was Wade's first cousin. She was down on her luck and took refuge with him and Margaret. She soon found there was no refuge there. Wade raped her after only three days and Wesley had seen the whole thing. He blocked Wade and the entire incident from his memory. However that affected his little mind is unknown.

Before Wade and Redding were able to get to their job site the rain started falling. At first it came in a sprinkle, then in a downpour. Wade was driving past Spooner's Café when the clouds opened. Wade jerked the steering wheel and skidded into the parking lot sideways. Wade chuckled as though he had done something funny then pushed Redding's head with his open hand in a playful gesture.

"Free coffee, I guess," he said.

"Free for who?"

"It's on me."

They went inside with Wade leading the way. Everybody in the place knew Wade. They liked him but knew his temper. When he wasn't drinking, he was congenial but when drunk he was one mean bastard. Wade didn't see himself as dangerous. He was cheerful with a warm smile and a playful attitude. If that one lone strain had been removed from his personality, he would have been a likable person. He was a hard worker and helpful to people in need. His problem was his degenerate sexual appetite and his low way of feeding it. When he preyed on children, he didn't consider how it might feel to them. He wanted satisfaction and beyond that there was no reality. He disassociated himself from his sexual conduct. He believed he was a good person. He could stand beside a child he had assaulted and threatened without believing his conduct had altered the child's fate.

Wade was a complicated man. As in his dealings with children so was his conduct when under the influence of alcohol. He could rampage and rattle and bang around verbally and physically and completely believe it was excusable because he was drunk. The rapist, the pervert, the drunk, those were other people who came out in dire circumstances. He was a good old boy with a big smile and a helping hand.

Today his mean streak would reign. Today that compartmentalized bastard who lurked behind his kind eyes and kind round face full of chaw would break out in fury and anger. Today was a day pregnant with misery and gloom. Without considering the wind and the rain and without considering the clouds so heavy they consumed the trees and the hills, and without considering the poor men who wore their skin like iron, or the rue hanging in the air, it would still have been dreary and mournful merely by being born by the dawn. It was a day that would go on too long.

After they had their coffee a bottle was passed around. Most participants sipped but Wade guzzled, and the bottle found its way to the trash before it found its way around the table. Wade slapped Redding across the back of his head and said, "Let's go."

The slap was intended as playful, but it was jarring.

"Hey, you son-of-a-bitch, that hurt!"

"Come on, cry baby," Wade ordered.

The rain was heavy, so they ran to Wade's truck. He slammed it into gear and floored it, spinning gravel as they went. Redding had barely made it inside the passenger seat and the door was swinging in the breeze. Redding was left with his legs hanging out beating against the wind. Wade laughed. He drove the narrow gravel road like a man possessed. Gravel was being strewn into the ditches and the wheel well was being hammered. Redding was pleading for Wade to slow down, but his pleas seemed to incite Wade into more reckless behavior. They turned a curve heading into Fremont and smack into a flooded low water bridge. The truck spun sideways and spewed water into the air but somehow it reached the other side still upright. Wade slowed down and partially recovered his senses. Wade smiled at Redding as though they were on a carnival ride.

It was only 8:30 a.m. but Sylvester's Tap and Café was full. The rain had shut down the loggers and the hog farmers and now they were lingering in the dank and dimly lighted taverns. Sylvester served breakfast, but alcohol was his main business. His beers were Stag, Falstaff and Budweiser. If you wanted something else, you went somewhere else to get it. Sylvester's wife and daughters were clearing tables but not quick enough to get beer to customers waiting with their rent money, and grocery money, and borrowed money, standing at the bar and sitting at tables clamoring for more haste in separating them from it.

Wade ordered two Stags, having two dollars in his pocket. Beer was 25 cents. Sylvester's daughters were 13 and 11. Sara Ann was the oldest and she was a pretty little brown-eyed girl, slender and quick. She popped around the tables hurrying to do as her mother told her to do. Wade watched her moving fluidly with little hands wiping tables and retrieving dirty dishes. His gaze was frozen on her. He forgot about the beer, the noise, Sara Ann's mother and he forgot about Redding.

Redding watched him, bewildered by what he was seeing.

"Hey, Wade, what the hell?"

Wade smiled.

"You know you're married to my sister, and if you ain't noticed, that there's a little girl!"

"Little girls grow up to be big girls, Redding." Wade said.

Redding just shook his head.

Wade paid for the beer and sauntered to the bar leaving Redding at the table. When his two bucks were nearly gone, he was sidling up to Redding again. Redding was eyeballing his billfold. He was almost broke too. Wade let go of his last 50 cents and ordered two Falstaffs. They sat alongside each other at the bar. Wade was more inebriated than Redding. He had been treated by several other customers who were on good terms with him. Wade had a government job and he usually had money. More often than not he was the one who treated others. Today there were paybacks.

It was nearly 1:00 p.m., and the tavern was starting to clear out. The noise and laughter had waned, and Wade was slumped over his beer bottle with elbows resting on the bar. He licked the bottle top, circling it with his tongue. Redding watched him with a twisted expression. He plunged his tongue in and out and moaned.

"Oh, Sara Ann, uhmm."

Redding was incensed. "You're a goddamned degenerate!" he said, scooting off his bar stool and started outside to the toilet.

While he was gone Wade thought about what Redding called him.

"A degenerate," he said softly, thinking about what it meant,

"A degenerate," he whispered. His brow furrowed. He pressed his tongue hard against the back of his teeth.

Finally, he spouted, "A fuck'n degenerate!" He was seething. He was a degenerate. He was a child molester. He was a rapist and his morals were nonexistent. Nobody knew those things better than he did, but the words hurt. There was pain behind his eyes, and all over his face. Just moments before he had become distraught by the accusation, he had licked a bottle intimating sexual desire for a child, humming her name, Sara Ann, Sara Ann. Now he was hurting but he didn't associate his behavior with the pain.

The pain became anger and it crept into his chest. He was tense and his teeth were clenched. When Redding returned and threw his leg over the bar stool, he had no warning of the beast in waiting. Wade stepped back and kicked hard against Redding's bar stool. Redding was instantly unfurled and left flat upon the floor. A swift kick landed a heavy boot and Redding was left gasping and groaning. Wade grabbed Redding's throat with a meaty hand. With anger and strength surging through him he picked Redding off the floor and dragged him to the tavern door and pitched him out into the rain.

The tavern was quiet. Shocked patrons watched Wade standing in the doorway with his chest heaving, his eyes wild, glaring and challenging anyone to comment. Even the hair on his neck stood, agitated like a huge angry dog. There were men in that beer joint who would climb 50 feet into a tree with a crosscut saw in one hand with nothing but the breeze between them and the ground, but looking into those eyes, none of them would hold his gaze. He stood and waited for a long moment then quietly picked up Redding's stool and returned it to the counter.

One brave soul went to the doorway and looked. He glanced back at Wade then meekly went outside. He helped Redding to his feet, and they walked together down the street to Gloria Jeanne's Tap. They didn't go for alcohol. Redding didn't need more alcohol. anyway, not the kind that went down the throat. He needed to be dry and he needed to recuperate.

Wade sat alone at the bar without anyone near him. Sylvester didn't ask if he wanted more beer, but he brought a Falstaff and popped off the cap.

"It's on the house, Wade, and maybe Margaret is wondering where you are?"

Wade knew he was being asked politely to vacate the premises. Sylvester wasn't going to force his hand, but he wanted Wade to know his conduct was unacceptable. In those small towns and counties, the bartender was the law. Every grown man was a beer drinker and the tavern, the social center. Wade's blood had stopped percolating and the Sheriff had spoken. He would drink his beer, locate Redding and head for home.

The rain had subsided to a steady drizzle, but the gutters were full, and the water ran over Wade's shoe tops as he splashed down the street toward Gloria Jeanne's Tap. His temper was doused, and he was feeling guilty for smacking Redding around. The clouds on the horizon were black and another pounding rain was on its way. Wade was drunk and he swayed and stumbled into Gloria Jeanne's.

Redding was sitting on a bar stool with the Good Samaritan who had fetched him out of the rain. Wade saw Redding's rifle propped against the bar beside him.

"Think'n about shoot'n somebody, Redding?" Wade stated lightly, trying to make up with him.

"Nope," he answered coolly.

The Good Samaritan spoke up, "He got his gun from your truck, Wade. I was getting ready to take him back to Wisdom's mill."

"He don't need you to take him back, I'll take him."

"I ain't going anywhere with you, Wade!" Redding snapped.

"I brung you, I'll take you!"

"And I said I ain't going anywhere with you!"

Wade stared at Redding. His ire was being stirred again.

"You started a bunch a shit with me, Redding. You got what was coming to you; now get in my truck and I'll take you back where I found you."

Redding slid off his barstool and backed up a few steps. His fists were clinched.

"I called you what you are, a God-damned degenerate. You sucker punched me! Now let's try it again!"

Without a word Wade proceeded to pummel Redding. He knocked him off his feet with the first punch then kicked and beat him senseless. The Good Samaritan tried to intercede, but he got thoroughly waxed too. Wade was so drunk he couldn't walk straight but the adrenalin had him so pumped his strength was increased and he was beyond control. Redding was saved from serious injury or death only because a group of mill workers came upon the fight and piled on Wade and held him until he stopped heaving and growling like a wild animal.

The Good Samaritan helped Redding retreat, bringing along his rifle as they escaped. Redding in a semi-conscious state muttered, "I'll kill that son-of-a-bitch if he hits me again."

There are days so long in misery they threaten to go on forever. This was a day defined by agony. The rain that couldn't end, and the long lingering parlays in dark, dank, dreary beer joints, and the men who were depleting their household incomes inviting more distress into their lives, and sting of anger and the burnt out feeling behind all their eyeballs, painted a picture of pending doom. If the night could have just come early and the lamps could have been lighted and their pillows gathered in their thoughts and silence subdued their fury, then the day would not have tumbled along until only the grave could quiet the rumble. But there was no relief. It was a day straight from Hell.

Redding went with the Good Samaritan and they licked their wounds together.

Redding bemoaned his relationship with Wade, commenting that he had never seen anything like it. He pitied his sister and wondered how Wade treated her when they were behind closed doors. Was he insane?

Wade staggered to his truck mumbling to himself for several minutes while men in the tavern stood in the doorway watching disapprovingly, but nobody ventured to caution him not to drive. He weaved along the street in his truck in the same manner as he had walked. He slowly ambled from one lane to the other as he left town at a snail's pace. He wandered into and out of ditches until finally his truck was buried in mud.

He cursed the truck then set out on foot. He walked in ditches with weeds and the wet grass thrashing against his overall legs until his feet were soaked and cold. He knew there was an old car in Richardson's hog lot. He had lingered there before watching kids going to and coming from school. He found his way through the field and crashed there in the back seat. The rain had stopped temporarily but he was completely depleted. He rolled onto his back soaking up the mold and hog shit and in an instant he was asleep.

Wade didn't know how long he had been passed out but when he awakened, he heard children laughing and shouting. He knew school was out. He felt refreshed. The sky was lighter, and the rain was gone, for the time being anyway. He watched several kids pass by, but his interest wasn't piqued until Irene Black and her sisters along with Wesley Finch were in view. It was then that he made a decision that would accentuate his obsession with unsavory results.

He hurried through the field and climbed over the barbed wire fence. He closed in on the kids in a hurry. The smaller children ran but the oldest stayed behind. He didn't intend to hurt her; he just wanted to take her into the weeds and do as he had done to several other children over the years. In his distorted reality, he had never harmed a child.

When he made his attempt, he found this one to be different. She fought like a caged wildcat. He was still very drunk, and she pushed him into the barbed wire fence. His overalls were laced with the barbs and his leg was cut open. He freed himself and sat there on the ground wincing over what a hell of a day it had been. He mopped the blood with the denim from his torn overalls then started walking towards Wisdom's mill with his rifle slung over his shoulder.

When he sauntered into the mill yard Redding was there with Lawrence Black. Lawrence was sitting on a log and Redding was on the ground with his rifle butted against a tree, the barrel pointing skyward. There were words between Redding and Wade. Obscenities and threats were exchanged. There were words between Wade and Lawrence. Little Wesley Finch had wandered into the mill yard and into the mill shed and was seated on the Sawyer's bench watching. Everything was cold and wet and except for the voices it was eerily quiet. Wesley listened as the quarrel escalated. Wade and Redding were agitated but Lawrence spoke with a calm and stern voice. At some point in time words were not sufficient, and in the end, there was fighting and gunfire. Wade was struck and went down. He rolled in the dirt moaning and crying then struggled to his feet and trotted across the skyline holding his guts in. He found his way to Lawrence's home and fittingly fell at the feet of his last intended victim.

A beam of light swept through the trees and the sun hovered on the horizon. The sky turned red and gold was effervescent in the clouds. A gentle breeze stirred the leaves and the sweet smell of honeysuckle was in the air.

Chapter XIII

Tom walked through the dining room surveying all the work he had done. The dining room had a new hardwood floor, a new ceiling, brilliant light fixtures and a fresh coat of paint. He looked through the French doors into the living room leading to the balcony and stoop he had made, and into the garden where he had built a fountain and laid flagstone. The prairie grass was swaying in the breeze and the day lilies, geraniums and mums were gleaming in the sunlight. He had to think he was a better carpenter than he was a writer. He was resigned at that moment to enjoy the things he had done, those things he could do well. He wasn't a writer. He was a former cop, now a paper pusher sort of a detective, and a fair businessman. He would never be the next Tom Clancy. There was no Great American Novel. He felt exhausted. He had finally come to terms with reality. *The Hung Jury* wasn't going to make him famous and the Great American Novel wasn't going to vindicate him for his lies and mistakes. He would just be happy with the irony and circumstance. He had been very lucky. A great big confession in print wouldn't make him happy.

As he had conceded the end to his folly the fax machine began to beep. He walked up the stairs admiring the beaded wains coating in the stairwell. He recalled how he had soaked it and molded it to the curvature of the wall, and it was perfect. The fax was still beeping so he went through the master bedroom and strolled through the double doors out onto the balcony. He recalled how he had reinforced the supporting joist with six-inch lag bolts and cut out supports with his compound miter saw. He remembered hacking through the exterior wall to find a permanent cross member to mount the header. When he closed it in there wasn't a beam of light that could get through. This was his forte. He would leave the Great American Novel to someone else.

Just then the fax buzzed, and he went to read it. Donna Webster had found the dead man article. She sent some other supporting follow-up stories as the calamity unfolded. The picture of Grandpa Black was included with him and Grandma Black standing in front of the courthouse. The dead man story was just as he remembered it. The final paragraph implied that it was Lawrence Black's gun that had sent the deadly bullet.

He placed the article into a manila envelope and filed it away. He glanced over the other follow-up articles. There was a picture of Eileen Finch with her little son Wesley Finch sidled up beside her. The article went on to explain that she was the widowed cousin who had lived briefly with Wade and his wife.

She refused to comment regarding Wade's character, leaving the reporter to infer that she believed he had none. Tom placed it into the manila envelope and filed it away.

As the evening progressed Tom ate cold broccoli and dip with cheese and grapes as he did every night. He called Molly and they discussed their day. Molly urged him to hurry and find a way for them to be together as she did every night. They ended the call with an "I love you," as always. Tom lay in bed in the dark looking at the ceiling. The neighbors' wind chimes were stirring, and crickets were clamoring. An occasional car drove past his home and brakes squeaked at the stop sign. He couldn't sleep.

At 2:20 a.m. Tom bolted upright. There was something wrong with the story!

Wesley Finch did not have a father! He remembered Wesley's comment, "My pappy told me to keep my mouth shut." The newspaper stated clearly that Eileen Finch was the widowed cousin of Jess Wade. What else was there about the story that wasn't true? At 2:45 a.m. Tom dressed and went to his car. It was a five-hour drive from Willoughby Hills to Fremont, Missouri. He felt foolish but who was to know except him? He had done stranger things. He had picked up a hitchhiker in Springfield, Il., and after hearing the man had terminal cancer and was trying to see the world before he died, he drove six hours in the dead of night to take him to Indianapolis, Indiana.

Tom stopped in St. Mary's Landing while en route to have breakfast with Glen, Joe and Jim. They didn't ask him where he was going. They already thought he was crazy by the way he traveled endlessly between Willoughby Hills and Mississippi and other places.

After another two hours he was in Fremont. He found his way to the bookstore and the barber shop. The bookstore was closed but to his astonishment a copy of *The Hung Jury* was displayed prominently in the front window.

"What the hell!!"

Anyway, he didn't have time to ask.

Wesley Finch was not on his bench. His son was gone too. An older man in a white smock was placing combs and scissors systematically on a white towel alongside porcelain bowls and barber chairs.

"Excuse me, sir, will Mr. Finch be in today?"

"No, he's down at Ironton at the hospital. His dad had a spell yesterday and he's down there with him."

"How far?"

"It's an easy hour from here, but he'll be there."

Tom was off again. He passed the bookstore and eyeballed *The Hung Jury* sitting there facing the street on a pedestal like a king reigning over the printed word.

"Unbelievable!"

It was less than an hour when he cruised into Ironton. There were three little towns there with about 1500 population in total, but they all had their boundaries. This street here would be in Ironton and that one in Pilot Knob and others in Arcadia. It was confusing and most people just called it Ironton, maybe because it was harder to pronounce, and they were amused by how people rolled into the word sideways. (try it, I R O N T O N)

As he walked through the hospital the anesthesia and cleaning fluids and kitchen odors mingled together to create that distinctive hospital stench. The weak coughing and the low droning from the breathing machines, and the quiet beeping were the sounds that whispered that you had arrived. They were odors and sounds that informed that you were in a place you didn't want to be.

Tom found Wesley Finch, Jr., sitting in a green vinyl chair outside the intensive care unit. He spoke to him quietly.

"Is your father alright?"

"He's resting. He's in no pain, but he ain't gonna make it."

"I'm sorry, I shouldn't have come."

"I figured you wanted to talk to him again about Lawrence Black. I know'd you was coming," he said, holding up his cell phone. "We ain't that backward down here." He ran his hand through his hair.

Tom hesitated as he debated whether it was really that important. Did he really need to know? Wesley Jr. stared at the floor. He waited for a long time before he spoke again.

"You know that old man's my hero. I've heard him say Irene Black was his little hero at least a hundred times. If she was your momma, and I think she was, she was surely something for you to be proud of. She surely was a good woman."

Tom was silent.

"My dad had a hell of a life, a hard life, and he's told me more times than I can count that the story you heard was the third most important thing ever happened to him, right behind me and my sister being born." Wesley Jr. stopped and wiped away a tear.

"He told me right from wrong. He always got his point across and he never raised a hand to me. I'd lay down my life for him, but he wouldn't let me."

Another tear dropped.

"I want you to go in there and talk to him but I'm staying here. He's already told me the story he wanted me to hear, and that's the one I'm taking to my grave."

Tom went into the room and took a stool beside the bed.

"Is that you Wes?" A small weak voice inquired. Tom thought again that he might go without pursuing the account further.

"No, Mr. Finch, it's me, Tom Webster."

"You're the one with the pretty wife?"

"I am, sir, I'm Lawrence Black's grandson."

"I figured you was. It seemed like you was a little shaky about my story the last time I seen you. You look like Irene."

"That's what they say."

"I'm glad you're back, Tom. As you can see, I'm about to meet my maker. I'm happy to be doing it too, but I don't want to go with a lie on my conscience."

"It's heaven for believers and eternal peace for non-believers," Tom said softly.

"Yes, sir, it is."

Tom waited.

Wesley opened his eyes and studied Tom's face. After he had examined every feature and every line, he closed his eyes and began to speak. "I've never told anybody this; you'll be the first to hear it. You can repeat it if you want but I wish you wouldn't, but you make up your own mind. I'll start with what happened after Jess Wade tried to grab your momma, cause all that was true, I lied about what came after that," he paused and took a few deep breaths. "After Jess Wade got out a that fence, he went up to Wisdom's sawmill. Your grandpa and that other feller, Scott, was there. He had a rifle on his shoulder and wobbled around a walking cause he was drunk. That's something I never done in my life. I hated seeing people gett'n drunk and mean. I guess that's why I never done it."

The story went on to depict an argument that had gone too far. Wesley indicated that he sneaked into the mill and sat silently watching. Wesley said he was nervous, but when he saw Tom's grandfather walk up between the two with their anger boiling, so strong and stern, he was reassured.

"Lawrence told them to settle down, and he meant it. Wade got all mean, and jerky, and stomped around, and threatened your grandpa, but Lawrence said, 'Wade you can kick dirt and spit and stomp around looking all wild eyed, but I'm a telling you if I see you in Richardson's hog lot, er anywhere else around that school I'll whup you like a mean dog.' He looked Wade right in the eye until Wade turned away.

Lawrence then went over to his truck and started working on it cause it was stalled out. He left his gun standing by a log. That Scott feller said,

'Lawrence, don't turn your back on him, he's a crazy s.o.b'—course he said the real words, but I won't say it being's I'm dying and all. Anyway, he said, 'Lawrence, he'll shoot you.'

"Your grandpa wasn't even worried. He said, 'Scott, he ain't got the guts to shoot a man, even in the back.' Well, after hearing that Jess Wade grabbed his gun and poked that Scott feller in the belly with the barrel a couple a times and he was laughing like he had lost his mind. Scott started running and I heard Wade close the bolt on his gun and I know'd it was loaded. I thought he was gonna shoot 'em both. Your grandpa was at least 20 feet away from his gun, so I jumped off the sawyer's bench and I run over there to get Lawrence's rifle to him.

I had it in both hands and I was running fast. I seen Wade shoot the first shot, and that Scott feller fired off a round too. I stumped my toe on a rock and I went down. It was like time was standing still. I could see fire flying out of Wade's gun, then I heard Scott's gun go off too, but the barrel was pointing up. I heard the third shot go off and I felt the kick when I hit the ground and I seen a flash go out the end of your grandpa's gun, and it was in my hand. I seen blood gushing from Wade's side, and he went down a moaning and a crying. I know'd it was me that shot him. It was an accident. I was praying he wasn't hit but I know'd he was.

"He got up and run but I knew he was gonna die. I was crying and begging God to help me and tears was a falling like rain. I kept saying, 'I'm sorry, I'm sorry.' I was nine years old and I was big for my age, but your grandpa came over to me and picked me up like a little baby and he held me in his arms and told me it was alright. He took me up to the mill and held me there for a while. He said that bullet was guided by God. He said it wasn't me that pulled the trigger. He said it was God's doing and God didn't make no mistakes. He put me down and told me to run off and never tell anybody what happened. I never did tell the whole story until just now."

Wesley would have stopped there, but Tom's open ears and forgiving heart were feeding his craving. A freedom that he had not known for a lifetime was growing with every word. "That Scott feller thought he shot Wade, and everybody seemed to think it was okay. Even the newspaper said it was Lawrence's gun that shot Wade, but nobody cared, not even Scott. They said it was a clear case of self-defense."

Wesley Finch lived for another 17 days before he gave up the ghost.

Tom never told Molly about his midnight rendezvous or about the final version of the dead man incident. He went back to Willoughby Hills and filed the articles he received from Donna Webster and tried to forget.

On August 15th he and Molly, along with Don and Lana, started their vacation at The Resort of Cocoa Beach where they shared ownership in a condo. It was located near the pier between Coconuts and Ron Jon's Surf Shop. The weather was beautiful. They were all soaking up the sun and Tom and Don were sipping Kahlua and coffee while Molly and Lana commented on every bathing suit that paraded down the beach. The sky was blue, and the waves were steadily lapping against the beach. Earlier in the morning one lone cloud meandered across the horizon hovering over the sea while a small funnel inched its way down until it dipped into the water. Tom and Don watched it totally mesmerized. The cloud was white on top, outlined in gold and black at the bottom. The sun shone across the low side and red streaks fanned out over the water. The deep blue sky behind it and the gray mist on the horizon all came together like a Michelangelo original. The little funnel bopped around for a short time then returned to its little hiding place above. The sun never stopped shining.

The Kahlua ran out and the ice bucket had become the dirty sandy water bucket, so Tom went back to the condo to replenish their supplies. They were equipped with a fax machine in the condo with internet service. While Tom was in the room the fax beeped and scrolled out a message from Ali. When he read it he smiled. Would the wonders ever cease? He placed the fax in his swimsuit pocket and returned to the beach.

They drank Kahlua until afternoon, then beer until the sun rays were casting long shadows down the beach. They all decided to walk to the pier and have Bloody Marys.

As they walked Tom marveled aloud at the amount of alcohol they consumed, and he didn't seem to be affected. Don had a ready answer. It was a sure thing he had considered it before.

"It takes us all day to drink a half bottle of Kahlua, a six pack and a bloody Mary. We used to do that in two hours."

"Yeah, I guess that's true."

They were quiet again. Molly and Lana were giggling, and Lana was leaning against Molly as they walked.

"That sure was some little tornado, huh?"

"Sure was."

"Like something in a movie."

"Yep."

They came upon two men lying passed out in the sand. They were unshaven and both had stringy matted hair. They were shirtless but were wearing dirty blue jeans with the legs rolled up to their knees.

One man's hat was screwed on tight, but the other's hat was nearby with two Budweiser cans holding it down. His face was nestled in the sand with grime and seaweed clinging to his scalp. They had two empty Bud cases brimming with empties.

"I guess they didn't need a cooler," Don said."

They both laughed.

Other normal looking beach goers had surrounded them and paid as much attention to them as if they were two pieces of driftwood.

"Ah, a day at the beach."

"Yep."

They laughed again as they stepped over them.

They finally made it to the pier. As the sun touched the horizon, they discussed the fact that once the red ball made contact with the water it would be three minutes until it was gone, or was it five minutes? They decided they would time it to be sure. Don checked his watch then forgot it as they had done numerous times before. Soon it was dark and the lights along the beach shimmered through the clear air while the silver moon glistened on the waves. The Bloody Marys were gone, and the foursome strolled on the beach towards their condo. Just as they were coming to the end of the light from the pier, Molly started jogging slowly, just barely quicker than a walk. She giggled a little then picked up her pace.

Finally, she took off in a dead run. Her long hair was drifting in the breeze as she kicked up her heels. The soles of her feet were visible, lightly churning the sand. She disappeared into the night like a ghost or a phantom. Tom laughed and started after her. Don and Lana joined in.

"Where's she going?"

"I don't know."

They were at least two miles from where they had left the blanket and cooler. Tom thought he would find her somewhere along the way, resting with her sandals in her hand. He jogged along; his breath was getting a little labored, but he wasn't quitting. As he came upon a little tiki bar just off the sand among the sea grass and bamboo, he saw a man sauntering towards the water. He was wearing red trunks, brown shoes and black socks. My god, it was Darrell Fox!

"Hey, Foxy, what are you doing here?"

"Hey, Tommy, how are you, buddy!"

"Doing good, Foxy, doing good."

Don and Lana had dropped out at some point and he and Foxy were there alone.

"I got a job here, Tommy. I start in two weeks. I'm gonna be the assistant to the regional manager of Fred's Department Stores. Have you ever heard of them?"

"Sure, Fred's are big here in the south."

"Yep, It's a good deal, Tommy."

"Number two, huh?"

"Well, number four, there's four departments, my deal is hardware, you know."

They were quiet for a long moment, both smiling and nodding their heads unnecessarily. Foxy was first to speak.

"You know about that last time I seen you at Juniors Tap, you know I, ah, ah," he stammered.

"Forget it Foxy, it's all good."

"It sure is, Tommy, it sure is."

"See you, Foxy, I gotta catch my wife. She's running down the beach. Good luck."

"Good luck to you, Tommy. Oh, I forgot, you Websters don't need any luck!

Tom looked over his shoulder.

"Just kidding, Tommy, just kidding!"

Tom jogged on and just like that, Foxy disappeared into the night.

When Tom reached the beach blanket Molly was face down. He plopped down beside her. She laughed and turned over onto her back. They both breathed heavily for a while. She wrapped her arm around his. He looked at her for a long time then fetched out the fax from Ali.

"*The Hung Jury* has sold a few copies," he said.

Molly smiled. They hadn't talked about *The Hung Jury* or *The Great American Novel* for a long time.

"How many?"

"They were all bought in one transaction."

"How many?"

"It was an internet transaction, bought and paid for in the middle of the night."

"How many?"

Tom smiled, was this irony, or was it fate?"

"How many!"

"One hundred thousand!"

"What! Who – how do you---."

"I know who did it." Tom said.

"Was it Bantam Books, or Barnes and Noble, or somebody like that?"

"They didn't say, but I know anyway. There were explicit distribution directives."

"Who was it, please!"

"It said to be distributed by Dollar Henry Stores, or to be incinerated behind the Dollar Henry Store, whichever was more feasible."

The End